Ashley Sprinkler: Ancient Sacred Twisted Journey

SHERLINA IDID

ASHLEY SPRINKLER: ANCIENT SACRED TWISTED JOURNEY

Paperback ISBN: 979-8848739343

Cover Designed by Miblart

Edited by Ashley Olivier Author & Editor and SnowRidge Press

Published by: Shariffah Norazlina Idid

To all readers,

dreams do come true.

Contents

THE EVIL GREEDY CAST

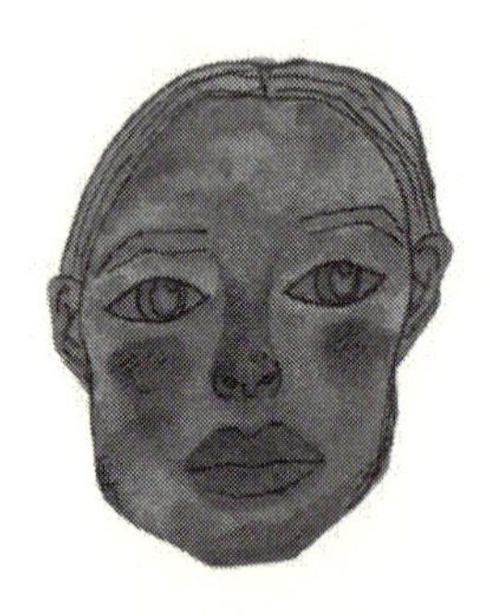

DANIELLE

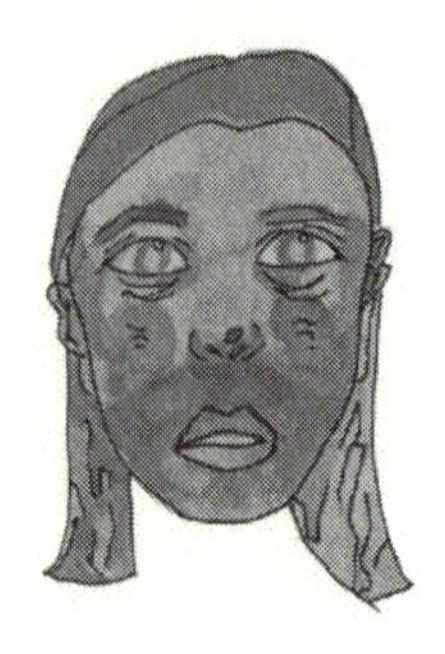

ANGIE

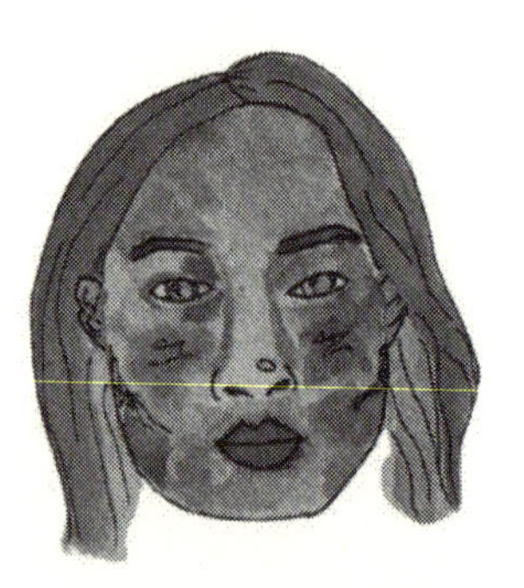

CINDY

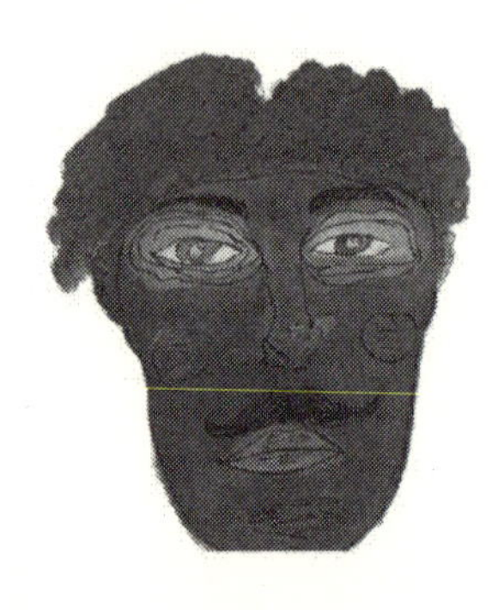

SPEED TWISTER

PROLOGUE

In the *Mystical Adventure of Ashley Sprinkler*, Ashley moved with her parents to her grandmother's cottage in Kuala Lumpur. A few months later, Professor Sprinkler continued pursuing the completion of a travel machine invention that was hidden at the secret laboratory behind the study walls. It was halfway built by Professor Augustine, Ashley's late grandfather.

Only Ashley's grandmother is aware of the existence of other realms due to her late husband and late Professor Sprinkler's journey and adventure that both shared with her. Since she has a close relationship with Ashley, as she is their only granddaughter, the girl knows the whereabouts of the realms.

Once Ashley's father passed away, she stumbled upon magical and digital artifacts, i.e the ring, bracelet, and magic sword that she uses to assist her during enduring adventures into four different realms with Bob and Dash (neighbour cats) and Billy the rabbit.

There are two kind-hearted realms: Tagu Tagu Realm, which comprises of good-hearted creatures named Cruelblocks; their features are like turtles and bodies are like stocky iguanas.

Next, the Goodness Realm is headed by Prince Jeff. It is a good-hearted kingdom full of magic, digitalisation, and high tech. The prince is also Ashley's friend, whom she met when she was mysteriously flown by the flickering lights journey.

There are two realms lead by evil witches and greedy creatures: Desperate Valley Realm, which is controlled by the Three Weird Sisters, and Maze Realm, which is governed and owned by Speed Twister. The Three Weird Sisters and Speed Twister's ultimate motive is to rule all the realms since they are thirsty for power, wealth, and recognition.

In addition, Mother Reddy, a naughty witch who lives in Coventry, United Kingdom, was placed under a spell by the Three Weird Sisters that has turned her into an enormous bird. She was held captive and has to adhere to the Three Weird Sisters' commands. Her daughter Val stayed with Ashley when Mother Reddy was held captive as they tried to find a magic antidote to save her.

Due to the greediness of power, The Three Weird Sisters were placed under a spell by Ashley Sprinkler's magic sword.

In this book, the story entails the undone spell/curse for the escape of The Three Weird Sisters.

CHAPTER 1

THERE ARE VARIOUS TYPES OF TRAVELLERS.

Thunder crashed, and lightning flashed. Then, sudden, heavy droplets of rain fell onto the ground.

Ashley, Billy, and Bob watched the sky from Ashley's grandmother's balcony at her house. Strong winds made a garden chair flip.

The fur on the back of the rabbit and cat stood on its ends. Ashley's dress felt that someone was pulling it hard in the garden's direction.

Witnessing this, three of them held hands, making a life rope, walking step by step by putting lots of effort and energy to withhold against the strong wind to enter Grandma's house.

One by one, they had to let go of their … one, two, three, four fingers, then the whole hands.

In the blink of an eye, they were absorbed into magical flickering light that appeared amongst the garden wall.

"Where are we?"

"Ni Hao Ma," said one lady.

Ashley smiled in return, not understanding a word she said.

Bob, Billy, and Ashley's eyes opened widely. They moved their heads from the ground, slowly turning upwards to see where they were. They were surprised to witness multi-coloured lights decorating the two-tiered sphere building.

"Woah! This building is tall, massive, and looks like two spaceships located at one structure at different levels," Bob remarked.

"Don't tell me we are in space!" Billy continued excitedly.

They all heard the sound of a camera.

"Excuse me, what are you doing?" Ashley asked the person beside her.

"I am taking pictures to remember this iconic tower." The person pointed their index finger towards the building.

"Why, and what is iconic?" Ashley questioned, confused.

The person waved at her. "Sorry, I have to go off to another tourist spot; my tour bus is about to leave."

Luckily for Ashley, a few feet from her, a boy who was five feet with a dimple on his left cheek and a straight-cut hairstyle had been listening to their conversation.

"Excuse me. Allow me to explain: It is because the unique architecture represents one of the sixth tallest towers in the world."

Ashley was astonished, her mouth falling open in surprise.

"Girl, you don't know its name?"

Ashley shook her head.

"Now, let me share with you the information; this is Oriental Pearl Tower/Shanghai TV Tower."

"Does this mean we are in Shanghai, China? It's amazing," Bob whispered to Billy.

"By the way, are you alone with your pets? I saw you appearing when the strong wind blew most of the visitors' hats away. Suddenly, three of you appeared out of nowhere," he said.

"You saw us suddenly appear at the foot of the pavement of Shanghai TV Tower when the strong wind blew?"

"Yes, I did. I was astonished since there are no vehicles visible nearby, and I did not recognise seeing three of you walking from any other sides of the Shanghai TV Tower."

"By the way, I am Ashley Sprinkler. The cat's name is Bob, and the rabbit's name is Billy."

"And my name is Lee Yi Chen from Shanghai, China. You are currently standing at the heart of the capital city. By the way, the dress you are wearing doesn't represent that you are from Shanghai. Where are you from?"

"We are from Kuala Lumpur, the capital city of Malaysia. We used to stay in England when my father, a professor, was alive. Currently, we are staying with my grandmother at her cottage."

"So, do spill the beans; how did you travel here? Was it by wind or magic carpet? It looks fantastic the way you appeared," Yi Chen asked while straining his neck to check whether Ashley was holding any carpet.

"It was magical," Ashley explained with a shrug. "First, I didn't know how it appeared out of the blue in my grandmother's garden with a magical flickering light. Then we magically arrived in your country. Maybe this auto ring and bracelet created the magical gateway."

While both were talking and the pets were staring and admiring the tower, a silhouette of a massive bird caught their eyes. It was adorned with red and brown feathers, wearing a small dark blue cloak over its neck. It had paws like a dog. It suddenly appeared within the thick clouds above the night sky a few feet from the tip of Shanghai TV Tower, flying rapidly downwards.

When the four of them looked at each other with their eyes blinking and then stared at the silhouette, suddenly it flew near to the ground. The four of them were appalled when it snatched Yi Chen by his jacket collar with its strong beak and then went up in the sky. It flew high above the Shanghai TV Tower.

Lee went up in the sky with the bird.

"Woah! Help! Help!" Yi Chen's face turned pale white as a ghost. His hands were moving here and there, trying to grab hold of anything to prevent him from falling.

The bird suddenly stopped, its wings flapping hard. Then its face bent down; its eyes looked at Yi Chen's face, then at his wrist, sparkling with excitement. Then it suddenly descended fast like a breeze, releasing Yi Chen from its beak at the height of twenty feet.

Upon seeing this, Ashley yelled, "Bracelet, please release safety net." While Yi Chen fell, the enormous bird's beak snatched his bracelet-like watch from his wrist in a flash. Yi Chen fell onto the safety net that appeared a few feet from the ground. He was lucky he wasn't hurt.

"Hey, come back, that's mine!" Yi Chen shouted while panting on the net, trying to get up to the ground.

The bird unlatched the bracelet watch with its sharp nails, leaving a long scratch on Yi Chen's wrist.

"Are you okay, Yi Chen? There is a nasty scratch on your wrist," Ashley said.

"Only my wrist is slightly injured. Otherwise, I'm fine. Luckily there was a net to save me from the fall," Yi Chen replied, straightening his jacket.

"My father will be furious with me for losing our family's ancient wristwatch. From generation to generation, the watch has been guarding us."

"This bird is so familiar … Do you think its features are like Mother Reddy of Desperate Valley?" Billy asked.

"Oh my God, you're right. It sure does resemble Mother Reddy," Ashley replied.

"I wonder what she's up to this time," Billy wondered, looking annoyed with his whiskers tilted aside.

"Do you know what hidden secrets of said watch are?"

Yi Chen shook his head.

"Follow me home, and we will get the first-hand story from my father," Yi Chen suggested.

Then he called for his transportation, which arrived within a few minutes just a few steps away from the spot they were standing.

Off they went in a chauffeur-driven car. A few minutes later, after passing some buildings and residential houses, they finally arrived at a large span of land holding an ancient Chinese architecture house with an emerald rooftop.

As they entered Yi Chen's house compound, which had an iron gate decorated with two dragons in green situated at each side of the gate, Ashley noticed that the garden had four neatly-trimmed bushes shaped like dragons, too.

Once the car parked at the entrance of the mansion, Ashley noticed the rooftop had a dragon statue with green and crimson red at each edge.

Then they saw a man in his thirties wearing a mandarin collar with a knot-button long-sleeve shirt in grey standing in front of the entrance door.

They quickly got out from the car, then bent their heads and waist as a respect and smiled at him.

"Huānyíng zuò wǒ de kèrén," Lee's father, Dr. Yao Yi Chen, greeted them.

"Hello, thanks for having us on short notice," Ashley replied, smiling as well as nodding in respect.

All of them stepped their feet inside the red heavy Chinese door, the entrance of Yi Chen's house.

Dr. Yao directed all of them into the living room; Yi Chen reiterated the recent incidents in Mandarin to his father.

"Dr. Yao, would you mind sharing with us the history of the wristwatch?" Ashley asked politely.

Dr. Yao raised an eyebrow and tightened his lips, his voice growing thick and unsteady.

"Yes, Ashley, the wristwatch has a magical element that protects my family from bad demons that have been haunting my family since the ancient days of our ancestors. My great grandfather, Xi Yao Chen, a shaman, was able to develop this protection magic. Due to its potent, powerful magic, unfortunately, if it falls into evil hands, there can be mass destruction."

"What causes it to be fatal? What power does it possess?" Ashley curiously said.

"Luckily, our ancestors were clever enough to ensure that the powerful magic would only work if two matching wristwatches lay side-by-side. But fortunately, only one wristwatch is relatively weak to release any tremendous power to do any grave damage."

Ashley considered this. "Who has the other pair of the wristwatch?"

"I believe it is with one of my ancestors who was buried in a graveyard in Beijing," Dr. Yao replied.

"I hope you don't mind me asking; I believe you have many ancestors buried, so which ancestor is keeping it?"

"All I know is that it is one of the four male ancestors that were buried; I would not know the details. However, I noticed that on your hands and left-hand index finger that you are wearing two ancient artifacts. I believe the artifacts you possess can detect the other pair of ancient magic wristwatches. It is just my hunch on the capability of your artifacts, but I may be wrong."

Ashley nodded in agreement; while they were discussing, all three of them could hear a sudden gust of strong wind coming from the outside. First, the neatly trimmed bushes outside the mansion swayed side to side. Then, the strong wind lingered at the bushes in order to give way to a harsher wind to pass through them.

The harsher wind knocked and pushed the mansion roof similar to a boxer pushing its opponents. This action caused the rooftop to shudder and eventually made some noises.

But the furious wind managed to enter the thick walls of the mansion; it refused to pass by but instead lingered at the guest room section of the estate, where Ashley and her friends were busy discussing.

Suddenly, it made a small tornado of wind in the center of the guest room. All four of them stopped discussing, turned their heads with eyes and mouth opened widely, overlooking the tornado.

"Oh no! Hold on tight, Billy and Bob!" Ashley screamed.

Seeing this, Yi Chen grabbed hold of Ashley's left hand while her right hand held the heavy antique Chinese cupboard in dark mahogany, pulling herself against the wind by using the cupboard as support. Her leg was standing firmly on the carpet. Her face became red with lines visible as she was using all her strength to pull herself away from the strong wind current.

Dr Yao pulled Yi Chen's body, then his waist, to prevent him from being absorbed into the strong wind.

"Yi Chen, let go of Ashley! Otherwise, the strong wind will take you away; you need to stay here safely; let Ashley and her friends save Earth from the evil creatures."

Obeying the wise word of his father, slowly, Yi Chen let go of Ashley's left hand and placed it onto the Chinese cabinet.

Ashley refused to let the wind to absorb her, but it was too strong.

During this time, her auto bracelet started to clash and chime frantically, making many noises; her ring shone frantically here and there on the ceiling and wall.

Dr. Yao raised his voice for Ashley to hear. "This sacred power requires combining the wristwatch with another wristwatch of its kind. The other three additional items holding ancient power were hidden in different parts of the world and may be hidden by other families. Please keep it safe within good hands!" Dr. Yao shouted at Ashley, who was slipping since she could not withstand the strong wind.

The current slapped repeatedly on both Ashley's hands; the pain was so unbearable that Ashley grimaced in pain and had to let go of the cabinet.

Once Ashley and the two pets disappeared within the blank walls, everything went silent at Dr. Yao's residence.

Yi Chen rubbed his eyes and started to touch the wall that Ashley and the others were absorbed into. He could not believe his eyes.

"Yi Chen, an ancient war is about to begin; Ashley and her pet friends are to save the world," Dr. Yao said. "From today onwards, let's pray to our ancestors to give

Ashley and her entourage bravery and victory against the evil spirit."

CHAPTER 2

All eyes were closed, as this time the trip within the magical gateway was harsh; the three of them were being jostled in the turbulent ride.

Ashley, Billy, and Bob maintained holding their hands even though their heads were spinning in the tornado, making them dizzy.

In a blink of an eye, all three of them rolled and bounced out onto a garden. *Splat.* They fell on their faces amongst the neatly cut grass.

"Where are we?" Bob asked.

"This garden has butterfly pea bushes with delphinium, along with hibiscus flowers just like Grandmother's. Look over there; it's our blue swing. In other words, we are home!" Ashley replied excitedly.

Bob and Billy high-fived each other's paws and danced.

Their happiness was short-lived, however, when a gust of wind swept up their fur. The strong current passed by; Ashley wobbled when she stood near the swing. Beneath them, the ground trembled. Cracks appeared bit by bit in the soil.

"Oh no, not again!" all three of them exclaimed.

Within seconds, the wind died. The garden grew quiet, and the breeze remained tranquil.

"What was that? I cannot determine which artifacts control or create the magical gateway. This is so frustrating," Ashley groaned, sighing loudly.

Ashley and the two pets were about to twist open the entrance door when loud shrieking voices came from the distance. The three of them looked over their shoulders toward the direction of the sound facing the Twin Tower, Kuala Lumpur City Centre (which could be seen from Grandmother's garden and balcony).

"Quick, close the door behind us and climb upstairs in your room," Bob told Ashley.

Once they entered the cottage, all of them tip-toed past the kitchen to Grandmother's tearoom and then to the main staircase. Their hearts beat rapidly.

Once the three of them were inside Ashley's bedroom, a bright ray of violet light shone through the dark grey thick curtain, consequently causing Ashley's room to be brightly lit.

Curious to know what the source was, Ashley flipped the curtain aside. Her eyes and mouth opened wide in shock. She was stunned upon witnessing the twin towers at Kuala Lumpur City centre—the multipurpose development area with shops, buildings, parks, and a fountain at the capital city of Malaysia—was covered with thick black clouds with lightning striking in between the building constantly.

At the same time, a loud shrieking noise came from the same direction.

"Where is the twin tower? Why can't I glimpse it? It was visible a few seconds ago, and now it is out of my sight." Ashley gasped and held her head, confused.

"What do you mean, where? It should be just there." One of Bob's paws was pointing in the same direction as Ashley's eyes were looking.

"Oh my God."

"I suppose the clouds of thick smoke are covering it," Bob exclaimed, covering his mouth with his paw.

"Oh, no! The clouds are clearing. I can see there is a silhouette of a huge bird with red wings flying forcefully between the tip of the two twin towers. It looks like Mother Reddy! What does she want from the towers?" Billy exclaimed while hopping up and down frantically.

"This is suspicious. Why must Mother Reddy come all the way from Desperate Valley Realm to Earth in Kuala Lumpur? I hope she is not doing anything mischievous. Let's go to the twin towers where Mother Reddy landed in order to prevent her from destroying or manipulating people at the Kuala Lumpur City Centre," Ashley suggested. Bob and Billy nodded in agreement.

Subsequently, Ashley took her sword kept in her dress pocket; since it had magic, it grew longer once Ashley held it in her hand. Then, she placed it above her head and muttered a spell:

Only the generation of true heart grants me with great strength.

Sprinkle with love, sprinkle with heart.

Let me be at twin tower Kuala Lumpur City Centre to guard its safety.

As she spoke, bright rays of purple and pink lights enveloped the sky just above her. Her brown hair curled, growing stripes of dark pink. Instantly, a pink filigree mask with rhinestones covered her face. In addition, her sword's pommel shone with white and blue light, which consisted of powerful good magic.

Out of the blue, with the sword's magic power, Ashley, Bob, and Billy appeared at the fountain entrance of the twin tower between Tower One and Tower Two of Petronas's office.

Upon seeing the twin tower building turned to darkness with its surroundings covered with several lightning bursts, a majority of passers-by ran frantically for shelter; mothers were carrying their children while running, pushing baby strollers as fast as their feet could carry away from the twin towers.

Some people fell while running when a gigantic fierce-looking bird with a height of 1,483 feet appeared floating side by side between both towers.

The giant bird landed on the pavement of Tower One, leaving a bunch of smashed trees and streetlamps in her wake. The ground trembled from her movement, and dust flew up from the ground.

Furthermore, passers-by witnessed a weird-looking man with his hair in the shape of smashed meatballs in bolognese colour with blue coloured skin on his whole face. He was standing sturdy on the pavement between the two twin towers. He held a shiny laser pen-like weapon.

He smiled as he looked at the fearful face of shoppers and onlookers.

"Hi! I am Speed Twister." He held the tip of his long, crooked moustache as he spoke to the panicked people running past him. His voice was boisterous with a high-pitched tone.

A man screamed, "Look! Look! A weird-looking man. Run! Run for your life! Monster invasion." More screams followed.

Ashley and the two pets appeared before the gigantic bird by using her magic sword to transport them.

"What is your aspiration, Mother Reddy? Why are you here in Kuala Lumpur?" Ashley demanded.

Speed Twister walked over until he was face-to-face with Ashley.

"My, oh my! How you have grown from the last adventure that I saw you, super Ashley." He winked at her mischievously.

Speed Twister replied on behalf of Mother Reddy, "Our purpose for arriving here is to collect items were hidden here. The items belong to my niece from Desperate Valley and myself from Maze Realm, dearie. We just recently found its location. It was left by our ancestors. We are not here to harm anyone. So, please stay clear. Otherwise, we will attack!"

With a flip of his magical laser pen, all onlookers and shoppers were unable to move a muscle. Only their eyes could move.

Upon seeing his hand about to flick his magical pen, Ashley concurrently managed to command her magical bracelet to protect Bob, Billy, and herself from being frozen.

"You are again lucky, dearie," Speed Twister said.

Mother Reddy started to flap her wings up and down, moving downwards gracefully and landing side by side with Speed Twister.

He hopped onto Mother Reddy's left wing, and then they sped away. She spread her enormous wings, pushing frozen people one by one, and crashed onto some trees as she flew up and up towards the tip of Tower One. Her size grew smaller and smaller as she gradually flew higher and higher to prevent destroying the twin towers that kept the sacred items they were searching for.

Before reaching the tip of the tower, they stopped momentarily on the outside of the sky bridge. From that spot, Speed Twister stood on Mother Reddy's strong wings, swinging his magical laser pen from left to right. He was about to cast a spell on all citizens within the vicinity of KLCC by circling himself.

Upon witnessing Speed Twister twisting and moving his hands using his magical pen, sensing something intriguing, Ashley Sprinkler, with the help of her sword, flew up to him.

"My, oh my! Look who's here trying to be a hero."

In the twinkle of an eye, Speed Twister shifted one of his magical pens towards Ashley. The powerful pen ray of evil light shone directly at the center of her stomach from where she was standing in the air.

Before it hit Ashley, she flipped over and said, "Bracelet, release protection shield!" The shield was a transparent light blue; no naked eye could see its existence, which concealed her.

Confident she was secured, she approached Speed Twister by striking her sword from upwards towards his direction. This action caused a strong wind to circle and blow around Speed Twister. He nearly fell off Mother Reddy's wing.

In a flash, his quick fingers grabbed hold of Mother Reddy's thick feathers. His muscular arms managed to pull him upright on Mother Reddy's left arm.

Mother Reddy saved him by flying away from the spot Ashley was standing. "Phew! Good old Mother Reddy, my savior. Let's go to the next tower to cause commotion to distract that nuisance girl so we can get the cure for my nieces," Speed Twister acknowledged.

On their way to Tower Two, as Mother Reddy flew past an empty pavement with several small fountains, one particular citizen caught Speed Twister's eyes. She was wearing a hijab in yellow; her two hands held onto two-tiered cakes with fruits decorating them. Speed Twister, who was mischievous, has chosen the particular lady. He pointed his magical pen at her, and instantly she turned into a minute size.

The lady flew up in the sky towards Speed Twister like lightning speed when he used his magic pen. She was waving her hands frantically as she passed. However, her hijab and cakes were still intact when she reached Speed Twister. He quickly pulled her with his long blue fingers. Speed Twister with the help of his magic pen created a Christmas ornament see-through glass with just enough space to fit her small size. He trapped her in a glass like a small birdcage.

"Come, Mother Reddy, let's fly past Ashley and show her who we captured. Our action will scare her; while she is trying to save this woman, we will get the sacred items in both towers without her noticing we're gone. Ha! Ha! Ha!"

Mother Reddy flew fast towards the outside of the sky bridge. She uttered a spell for her size to turn bigger than usual. This action attracted Ashley to come to her spot.

"Come and save her if you dare, Ashley!" Speed Twister shouted loudly.

Hearing this and seeing a hijab Kuala Lumpur lady trapped in a glass ornament, Ashley felt intense pressure to save said citizen and return her to her original size.

Ashley pointed her sword upwards, instantly reaching his spot. Speed Twister vanished into thin air, along with Mother Reddy. A gust of wind lingered after both of them fled.

Ashley gaped at the empty space in shock; she turned her body to the left and right searching for Speed Twister and Mother Reddy in the vicinity outside the skybridge to no avail.

"Speed Twister and Mother Reddy, show yourselves!" Ashley shouted. However, they did not reappear.

She extended her hand and shone her auto ring from one end to another to detect the whereabouts of both Speed Twister and Mother Reddy.

A few minutes passed, and her auto ring started to show two silhouettes: a bird and a man in a distance within the clouds.

With the assistance of her sword, Ashley could fly towards the silhouette. Once she reached the spot, both

Mother Reddy and Speed Twister, with his magic, were invisible from Ashley's vision. She breathed in deeply.

"Where are they, 'ring' and 'bracelet'? Are you able to detect both of them?" Ashley talked to her artifacts while breathing deeply.

It was a cunning distraction made by Speed Twister. He placed a spell on the clouds to make it look like both silhouettes. His magic tricked Ashley's ring.

Unexpectedly, Ashley's ears started to twitch when a loud metallic clang ringing in the air. She could hear the menacing sound coming from both towers. She saw a huge hole form in the tip of Tower One. Speed Twister must have ripped off the Tower One spire with estimated five meters. Then she turned to look at Tower Two; it shared the same fate as Tower One.

Mother Reddy and Speed Twister had taken something sacred hidden from both towers.

"They fooled me!" Ashley exclaimed with anger burning through her veins.

I wonder what it is that they are searching for and why? Ashley thought to herself.

"Why am I holding a stick facing towards the sky?" one of the passers-by asking loudly while blinking his eyes. Suddenly, all citizens and shoppers returned to normal and forgot the earlier incident. They even forgot that Speed Twister cast evil magic on them to freeze.

"Unbelievable. They zapped their memory!" Billy gritted his teeth.

CHAPTER 3

"Look, sisters, Witch Z is wearing a beautiful, powerful necklace set with diamond and ruby. The stones are believed to gives her the greatest power that she desires. As long as she owns the powerful necklace, she is the most powerful witch in these whole five realms, as well as in the universe and Earth!" Danielle shouted with her eyes green with envy while overlooking Witch Z through their crystal magic ball.

Danielle, with her skinny fingers, tried to grab hold of Witch Z's necklace through their crystal magic ball. The magic ball was covered with Danielle's fingerprints, which obstructed the clear view of the magic ball.

"Argh! My power is limited; I cannot grab it via the crystal magic ball!" Danielle exclaimed, walking from her royal seat to the next seat, and then climbing down the marble staircase. She fidgeted her fingers while walking to and fro.

"My, oh my, sister. No witches in the universe or realms can ever steal from each other via the crystal magic ball; its purpose is for us to spy on each other." Angie chuckled.

"I don't think that is the only item that makes Witch Z the most powerful witch in all the realms and universe," Angie elaborated.

"Look, she is holding something long and gold. Oh, it is a long rod. No, it is a scepter. Its tip has a symbol of a rose surrounded by a crouching dragon, which has an amulet on the dragon's eyes; it is a ruby, too!" Cindy looked at the crystal ball earnestly to make out the intricate details of the scepter.

"In conclusion, we have to take the scepter and the ruby necklace to conquer the whole universe and realms, and we will make all the community bow down at our command!" Danielle shrieked.

"Let the conquest begin!"

The Three Weird Sisters, Danielle, Angie, and Cindy, twisted and turned their magic fingers above their heads.

Their action released evil magic, which turned them into princesses with long dresses in velvet with laces trailing in the center in a zig-zag pattern. Tiaras were on all their heads.

"We are ready to attend the ball of the year organized by Witch Z. Tonight will be a night to remember, as we will capture and trap Witch Z in the snowball ornament!" Danielle smiled.

Angie and Cindy chorused, "I wonder how we can turn Witch Z into our servant with our magic?" Angie placed her index finger under her chin.

"My sisters, we have to steal the necklace set and scepter to make our plans materialize."

The invitation to the dinner gala extended to all witches in the various realms. The gala was an appreciation event for the collaboration of all witches, both good and evil.

Three of them were laughing and smiling, excited that they would be attending the gala. They imagined their success in conquering the Zamrud Realm once those two items were stolen.

The three of them planned to transport to Witch Z's realm magically; they twisted and turned their magic fingers to release magic, and then they were flying above the sky of their mansion when suddenly something hard hit their heads.

"Ouch, that hurt! Why can't we go beyond Desperate Valley Realm? It feels that there is hard object preventing us from leaving," Angie said, annoyed while rubbing her forehead.

"Let's try again."

Unfortunately for them, three of their heads knocked against something hard; the texture felt like steel mixed with bricks.

"What is the meaning of this!" Danielle's face turned cherry red; her strained vein could be seen on her neck, and her eyes looked like they would fall from their sockets.

"Wait, let me feel the sky of Desperate Valley." Cindy immediately took off the white embroidery gloves she was wearing and extended her hands, touching the surroundings. "I can feel the powerful force pushing my hands downwards. It is so powerful that my magic is unable to withstand the forcefulness of this power."

All of a sudden, a small lightning blasted off on Cindy, burning her right hand, causing her to tumble down from the sky and fall on her face on the muddy grounds.

Danielle and Angie quickly flew towards their sister's side; the forces burnt her face, and her chest was moving slowly up and down. Seeing her breathing, Angie wriggled her five fingers to revive her sister from the sudden electric shock as well as renew her burnt skin. Her breathing regulated.

Angie saw Cindy's mouth moving. "Are you trying to say something, Cindy?"

Cindy whispered, "Ashley's protective magic is strong; we need to find an antidote to escape." Then she closed her eyes.

Danielle instantly shoveled her magic fingers and made Cindy disappear. "She will have a good rest in her bedroom. My crystal magic ball, come to me," she commanded. Within a few seconds, it appeared in front of her and Angie.

"Show me Speed Twister, and command him and Mother Reddy to attend an emergency meeting this instant!"

***

Speed Twister spoke into his magic ball shaped like a lollipop, "You summoned me, my lovely nieces? What can I help you with this time?" he smiled.

"We are trapped in our own realms. We tried to fly through the sky to attend Witch Z's gala; however, there is a force pushing us down. Then it even burnt Cindy's face. If we are unable to go out from our realm, this means that we are unable to kick off our conquest plan! I want to kill Ashley Sprinkler!" Danielle stomped her feet with her fist at her side; instantly, her lips curled.

"My, oh my! You don't look pretty when you're all fierce and frantic, Danielle. Remember that in every pain, there is a solution. We will do this together as a team. As a family," Speed Twister soothed Danielle. "From the description of you being unable to go beyond your realms, I think that Ashley's magic sword planted a curse on three of you." he added while placing his right hand on his chin.

"But uncle, the gala invitation to Zamrud Realm is the only way for us to enter Zamrud Realm. We will never get this chance again!" Cindy shouted and slammed a table beside her.

"My nieces, there is a secret passageway to enter Zamrud Realm; it is through the underworld, and it just so happens that I know someone there who can help us when the time is right." Speed Twister twirled the tip of his moustache.

***

In the Maze Realm library, Speed Twister hid for hours and hours; days turned into nights. He was searching for the complete antidote to the curse.

One day, as he was hurrying after a delicious breakfast, he stumbled upon a chess look-alike flooring. His face splat on it; then, he felt the floor shudder for a few seconds, which led to an opening on the flooring just in front of his face.

Curiously, he said, "What an interesting passageway. Let me check this out." Without any hesitation, he pushed the floor aside just enough to fit his skinny, frail body into it.

The steps were uneven, and its rails were covered with thick dust as he passed by. He could see sticky spider webs hanging beside the staircase wall, and it was dark.

Speed Twister switched on the torch he grabbed from his pocket, which illuminated a huge painting hanging proudly on the wall opposite the landing of staircase.

He read the wordings on the painting, which indicated:

"Anyone who sees me,

Your wish is my command."

The painting had a huge tree with a baby centipede with tiny spots on its skin. As he came closer to look at the painting thoroughly, it changed to an enormous centipede skull. The transformation made Speed Twister fall back in surprise.

"Well, I guess it would not hurt for me to wish. I need to know where to find the ancient sacred elements buried to break the curse befallen on my nieces, the Three Weird Sisters."

In a flash, magical writing appeared on the painting canvas.

"The magical items are hidden in famous countries on Earth."

"Thanks so much." Speed Twister ran at top speed, climbing up the staircase. "I better not waste any more time. I have to start the search by going to Earth with Mother Reddy."

Speed Twister stopped momentarily when he felt a strong arm pulling him firmly from his waist, withholding him from running away.

He heard an echo coming from the painting, "There is a price to pay for the information. You will be my servant once your nieces are free."

Speed Twister's eyes open widely at this covenant.

"Let's discuss this as gentlemanly as possible; for how long, and what am I to do if I am to obey you?"

"The only way for me to escape this painting is for you to get hold of the magical sword that Ashley Sprinkler possesses. But unfortunately, that sword has placed a curse on me; I have been trapped here for over a hundred years!"

"The secret you shared is not an antidote to your escape, Mr. Magical Spirit?" Speed Twister asked.

"The secret is specifically for your niece's scenario. Mine is a more complicated situation. Placed by none other than Professor Sprinkler."

"As I thought. Well, it is a promise. So, it will be a win-win situation," Speed Twister replied with a smile.

***

A few days later, a crystal magic ball was shining and blinking while the Three Weird Sisters were having a serious discussion on reviving the glory of Desperate Valley.

"Danielle, me and the Maiden of Maze for the past few days were searching for an antidote to undo the curse befallen on the three of you," Speed Twister commented.

Danielle responded, "A curse? Not a spell? No wonder it is so fierce and unbeatable."

"You are quite true there. But listen carefully. I will need to go to a journey to planet Earth to locate the elements of ancient items; they are hidden in parts of the renowned world. I suggest that Mother Reddy and I lead this task since we require her strong paws and claws to snatch the precious ancient elements. Also, only creatures from the Maze Realm are able to enter and exit Earth easily." Speed Twister's eyes looked earnestly at Danielle.

"That is true. Go ahead with her!" Danielle shouted with her hands splayed widely.

CHAPTER 4

Two shining items blazing from afar blinded Danielle's eyes. She covered her eyes with her right hands, then smiled.

"You got the sacred items from Shanghai and Kuala Lumpur, Uncle and Mother Reddy. I am proud of your accomplishments," Danielle clapped her hands while standing on her royal seat decorated with a touch of golden trimmings.

"Good job, chap," Angie added, clapping her hands.

"So, what are we to do with both magical items?" Cindy asked.

"I am repeating it for the hundredth time that these items will release us from Ashley Sprinkler's magic, which holds us captive within our realm!" Danielle shouted to both her sisters.

"Give me those items at once!" She felt frustrated from being trapped within her realm for months and months, unable to venture into other realms or the universe to conquer more magic, power, and wealth.

"Firstly, how do you know about the sacred items and the countries we went to?" Speed Twister asked.

"Thanks to our magic crystal ball, we were able to track you and Mother Reddy's whereabouts," Danielle explained.

"Looks like my nieces are impatient. Of course, you may have the sacred items found from Shanghai and Kuala Lumpur, but with one condition: I will be your second in line to the throne." Speed Twister laughed while touching the tip of his moustache.

"What throne? Which realm or country are we conquering?" Cindy asked.

"You will see it soon once we escape from this misery of being prisoners!" Danielle's voice turned unsteady, shaking with anger.

Achoo! Achoo!

Angie alighted a small ball of fire at the tip of her fingers in self-defence. The fire moved fast like lightning towards the sound.

Speed Twister manoeuvred the small glass ornament aside for the fire to miss hitting the thing.

"I have captured a human being and made her small. She appears to be a baker for outstanding eye-breaker cakes," Speed Twister replied. "She will be our subject just like Mother Reddy."

Cindy added, "A slave for sure!"

The human pleaded, "Let me go, please! I will bake anything for you."

Danielle came closer to look at the human baker. She snapped her fingers to get a hold of a magnifying glass to look at the baker, who was a small size.

"I see … a lady baker with a cake decorated with fruits. Hmmm, at this very moment, I only know Witch Z loves eating cake with fruits. So, this woman will benefit us for our strategy to conquer."

Her magical finger pointed directly at the human baker, making her appearance change to a short and plump tummy wearing a yellow chef uniform with a dark, blue-striped apron.

"An additional appliance of a wooden rolling pin in your left hand will make you look an elegant royal baker," Angie added while she placed her magic finger in the baker's direction, which created the rolling pin in the blink of an eye.

"So, share me with your plans, my dear uncle," Danielle requested. "I am eager to hear your plans on our conquest, of course, after we obtain our freedom." She rolled her eyes.

"We will utilize the baker in our conquest to one of the realms. Meanwhile, I will keep her in the snowball ornament and place it amongst other Swarovski crystal collections of yours. We are using this method to prevent easy detection by the nuisance kid Ashley Sprinkler." Speed Twister chuckled.

***

Danielle smiled, uttering a spell while two of her palms faced upwards. Then she twisted both palms to face the floor, which was located five hundred feet from her royal seat.

Her action made the marble floor shake slightly, and then a rotating table appeared in the center.

"I will make a magic crystal bowl appear at the centerpiece." Danielle's eyes focused on the bare square table with thorns surrounding it. She twisted and turned both her hands, and the magical crystal bowl appeared in midair, twirling with slight greyish smoke accompanying it. Finally, after bending and curving, it settled at the center of the table.

"Come, Speed Twister, give me the two magical elements."

"Here goes, a wristwatch from Shanghai and two tips from Tower One and Tower Two of Kuala Lumpur Twin Towers."

Speed Twister took both items from his dark violet velvet jacket hidden in his front pocket using his magical pen.

Danielle impatiently pointed two of her skinny index fingers from both hands towards the item in Speed Twister's left palm. She snatched it from him.

Instantly, a ray of orange light emerged from both of her fingers; the lights circled both items, grabbing them firmly. Once secured, Danielle moved her fingers into the center direction.

The two items moved along with the ray of orange light into the center.

Danielle carefully maneuvered both items and placed them beside the magic bowl.

"I will place item by item first. The ancient wristwatch from Shanghai that has the strength of the ancient fighter dragon to be placed first. Then mixed with my potion from the underworld," Danielle said while her eyes turned to emerald green.

"Let the transformation begin:

All the ancestors from Shanghai
I am your warrior.
I am your queen.
Bow to my command.
Release us from the curse!"

After the potion and the ancient Shanghai wristwatch combined, a silhouette of a fierce dragon with red eyes and its skin rough like a crocodile reptile appeared. The colour of its skin was old red intertwined with jade green.

It released a ball of fire from its massive mouth in Danielle's direction.

Angie was quick to respond.

"Lalalalilililop Fire to be the death of you." Angie quickly uttered the spell. Her right index finger with evil magic pointed in its direction to prevent the bolt of fire from hitting Danielle.

Suddenly, the fire turned to a puff of smoke, which released into the air.

"Phew! That was close," Danielle muttered under her breath.

Speed Twister pointed his magic pen towards the wristwatch located in the bowl. He shifted it out from the bowl and slowly placed it on the table.

"Danielle, these ancient sacred elements are to lay side by side, never to be separated during the ritual session," Speed Twister advised with a sigh. "Next time, please be patient until I have shared with you the processes. I learned it from the witchcraft university." He kept the truth to himself. He was not sharing the covenant that he did with the magical spirit.

Cindy remarked, "The ancient dragon must be furious that you woke him up and asked him to bow for you. He must have been sleeping for years and years."

"We have to be cautious and sensitive to the rituals procedures and awareness of its cultures when combining the power of ancient tradition from various parts of the world," Speed Twister added.

"Let us place the shining tip of the ancient element from KLCC Tower, along with the ancient wristwatch, side by side in the crystal bowl, then pour our potion of greed onto them to restart the rituals," Danielle suggested.

"Hold on, let's gather further information on these two elements before we restart the rituals," Speed Twister responded.

Speed Twister twisted his magic pen clockwise twice, and then a book with a sprinkle of magic dust appeared in front of him. It floated in the air, waiting patiently for Speed Twister to turn its pages.

"Let me see the table of contents in this book, magic from the 'Tanah Melayu' (Malaysian) royalty; it is not written anywhere in this book. Let me flip to page 2,500 to learn about the ancient wristwatch. Here it is … The powerful dragon that grants one wish will wake up peacefully if mixed with other tranquillity elements. Now, turn to page 260, tranquillity for the powerful ancient elements." Speed Twister's eyes were looking directly at Danielle.

"For any witches in any realm to be free, it is compulsory for the ancient sacred elements to be side by side with another source of power. Only the ancient elements can recognize which elements they can match with."

Then the magic book coughed out words in the air written in clouds. *The ancient Chinese wristwatch was powerful when combined with its identical wristwatch. It was so powerful that it could cause a grave destruction to all creatures including witches and humans.* Then the sentences vanished into the air.

"So, in other words, my dear nieces, there is no straightforward answer to free all three of you."

Danielle jumped up and down, screaming her head off around the spot nearby her royal seat. "I will destroy you, Ashley Sprinkler and Prince Jeff, the leader of Goodness Realm!"

"There is no harm for us to try to combine these two elements. If we are lucky, both are compatible with each other, and we are free in no time," Angie said optimistically.

"Okay, Angie and Cindy, let's do this together!" Danielle commanded. Both nodded.

The three of them surrounded the table with a magical crystal bowl located in front of them, and they ensured that they were eighty feet apart from the bowl. This was in a preparation for any adversity that may arise during the initial ritual.

"One, two, three!" They all raised their palms facing upwards; they began to flip their palm upon reaching midair above their chest. Then, their skinny index fingers pointed at the two sacred items placed beside the bowl. The two items moved gradually towards the magical bowl.

Then Danielle uttered a spell. "Arbralililoath."

The spell caused a gust of wind to pass by their faces; a twirl of wind, along with small lightning, was released from the bowl.

The fierce dragon silhouette appeared, this time larger than before, and a distorted lady in white with long black hair rose from the bowl.

"Berani kau memanggil ku daripada tidur!" (Brave of you disturbing my peaceful sleep). The lady's eyes turned bloodshot, and her hand, as old as toad skin, clasped

Angie's neck tightly, causing her to choke. She scrambled to pull her grip off to no avail.

Quick thinking, Danielle released her magical power to the lady in white. However, it did not deter her hands from gripping Angie's neck.

Seeing this, Speed Twister, with his magic pen, touched the lady in white's hands, burning them as two magical sources from Danielle and Speed Twister were able to scald her fingers, and then she finally released her grip on Angie's neck. She coughed, while her body slumped, and next, she let out a sigh of relief.

Cindy came close to her and hugged her for comfort.

"Mr. Dragon and Lady in White, please, we are here not to be an enemy but to offer a truce."

"What do you want from us?" The dragon grew bigger with its face turned red, and the white lady's fingernails grew longer and sharper.

"This dreadful curse traps us. Please … please help to release us." Danielle knelt with her forehead touching the ground, showing respect and seeking forgiveness from the two ancient magical spirits.

The two spirits shifted their positions, moving closer to Danielle. Then both circled in the air above her head.

They said in unison, "Let us touch all three of your heads for us to feel the greatness of the curse."

Danielle, Angie, and Cindy all nodded in agreement.

Angie and Cindy knelt beside Danielle's spot.

The dragon and the lady in white touched all three foreheads simultaneously, then both shuddered in despair.

"Argh!" the dragon and lady exclaimed together. "The curse on your body is too hot … too powerful … We cannot penetrate nor command it to be dispersed. You need to find two additional sacred elements in a different shape and design, hidden in a remote area in other continents of the world." With that, they disappeared.

'What are the other two sacred elements, and where are they hidden?' Danielle asked.

Speed Twister answered, "My dear niece, don't worry. Mother Reddy and myself will find the other two elements."

Then he thought to himself, *Where can it be?* He twirled his moustache, thinking.

Mother Reddy was standing at the mouth of the entrance of the room, and she overheard the conversation and Speed Twister asking himself.

"Oceania, America, South America, and Europe, here we come." Mother Reddy chuckled at Speed Twister, standing sturdy as a phoenix cum Simurgh bird.

"Let's go, Mother Reddy! We have no time to waste in finding the balance ancient sacred items!" Speed Twister replied.

CHAPTER 5

"I must rescue the lady Speed Twister took!" Ashley said to Bob and Billy.

"Let's return home and visit Prince Jeff; maybe he has the antidote for your leg as well as a plan for these mysterious events."

Ashley took her sword, which was leaning against her thigh, and shifted above her forehead as she muttered a spell:

Only the generation of true heart grant me with great strength.

Sprinkle with love, sprinkle with heart.

Let me be at my grandmother's cottage.

Once they arrived, they quickly climbed upstairs to her late father's study room at her grandmother's cottage in Kuala Lumpur. Val was in the secret laboratory testing her magic. Ashley entered and related the incidents to Val.

"Would you like to join me to the Goodness Realm?" Ashley asked.

"No, please go ahead without me. I am trying to finalize a potion to reverse the Three Weird Sisters' spell on Mother Reddy," Val responded.

"It's fine. Please go ahead with finding the antidote to reverse the wicked spell. I am glad each day that you are close to finding the antidote." Ashley hugged Val.

"Are you ready, Bob and Billy, for an adventure?" Ashley asked them with a smile. They both nodded in excitement.

Then Ashley took her sword above her head while throwing the white handkerchief that Prince Jeff from Goodness Realms gave her and uttered a spell:

Only the generation of true heart grant me with great strength.

Sprinkle with love, sprinkle with heart.

Transport us to Goodness Realm.

Poof.

All three of them appeared in the garden neatly arranged in a maze. There were four-season hydrangeas, such as oakleaf, smooth, panicle, and beautiful bigleaf hydrangeas. Fernleaf bleeding heart flowers were also scattered everywhere.

"Hello, Ashley. Fancy seeing all of you here. How have Ashley, Bob, and Billy been?" Prince Jeff greeted all three of them.

"Hi, Prince Jeff!" Ashley smiled and waved her hand while Bob and Billy hopped up and down.

"I can see that something is troubling you, Ashley. Your face does not appear to be smiling. There are worried lines written on your forehead. This is not the face of the cheerful little girl that I met the first time. Please tell me if I can be of any help," Witchery Minister expressed.

"Spot on," Billy affirmed.

"Amazing! So, you can read people's emotions and fear," Bob thought out loud.

***

The sun fell below the horizon, allowing night to take over and stars to dot the sky. Prince Jeff invited his guests for dinner in the main dining hall.

While all of them were indulging in delicious food from the royal kitchen, a rectangular box suddenly appeared from the mantelpiece on the left side of the dining table.

It automatically screened updated news on politics, the environment, and citizens from several countries and realms.

"Wow, this is cool. So much news from various parts of the world and realms simultaneously broadcasting," Bob said.

"Let me change the channel to concentrate specifically on planet Earth news since I noticed a red light blinking on the Earth section, which indicates that there is trouble," Prince Jeff said, pressing the remote control.

"Red alert, red alert, a strange phenomenon is happening. There is a collision of weather, and thick ice is melting fiercely, causing massive flooding in the Antarctic. Also, we received a report that the Eskimo Igloos located in the residential areas are melting bit by bit, making people homeless."

"Within a day, the sun's heat tremendously changed. Normally, the igloo area, road and trees are shrouded with thick snow. Therefore, the thick snow prevented any heat from touching our skins. Only sunlight was visible. However, yesterday I could feel the scorching heat on my bare skin." The Eskimo related his experience to the newscaster. The screen showed sea lions and seals perishing in the heat.

"Look! A bird! A huge, beautiful bird with red feathers and a blue cloak covering its neck was seen flying above the Antarctic."

Bob exclaims, "It's Mother Reddy! What is she up to disrupting that region?"

In a flash, Ashley took her sword above her head and was about to mutter a spell when she felt a firm grip pulling her hands away.

"Ashley, we must not act foolishly. We must strategize and not go without any plans," Prince Jeff scolded. "I suggest that you and I go. Witchery Minister and the pets will remain in the Goodness Realm."

"I agree with your idea, Prince Jeff," Ashley responded. "In order not to miss the opportunity to meet and gather some information from Mother Reddy, why not go now?"

Prince Jeff nodded.

Then Ashley placed her sword above her head in mid-air to take Prince Jeff in this rescue mission.

She uttered:

Only the generation of true heart grant me with great strength.

Sprinkle with love, sprinkle with heart.

Transport me and Prince Jeff to the Antarctic.

As she spoke, her outfit changed. This time, it was according to the climate, a thicker clothing, as the Antarctic was colder than the Goodness Realm. Her top was a short sweater in pink with a woolen skirt covering her long legs.

In addition, her sword's pommel shone with white and blue light, too bright that Prince Jeff had to close his eyes.

In the blink of an eye, Ashley and Jeff landed on a piece of thick ice that was illuminated by the sun. Already, they could see it was melting.

Ashley felt a sudden gust of wind. *Zoom … Zoom.* A huge red bird flew past them.

The strong air caused Ashley and Prince Jeff's hair to go up in the air.

Ashley called out, "Wait, Mother Reddy, let's discuss this!" She raised her sword, pointing it straight at the giant bird.

Her sword magic froze Mother Reddy's wings. Only her eyes were moving and blinking.

In a flash, Mother Reddy was frozen.

Suddenly, a cackle sound could be heard hiding behind Mother Reddy's thick feathers, and then Speed Twister jumped down from Mother Reddy's huge left wing. He landed on the melting pavement a few feet opposite from where Ashley was standing.

"My, oh my, look who is here having a vacation." Speed Twister fidgeted his fingers while holding the tip of his long curly moustache. "Why are you surprised to see me? I will tag along with Mother Reddy as long as I have not found the ancient sacred items."

Ashley glared at him.

"Speed Twister and Mother Reddy, we would appreciate it if you would inform us why you have decided to melt Antarctica," Prince Jeff said professionally.

"I am giving you a hint that I require to find the balance ancient sacred items believed to be hidden on Earth in order to release the curse that Ashley's sword planted on my nieces!" Speed Twister replied before suddenly running away and hastily taking his magical pen from his jacket pocket.

Ashley noticed his movements and immediately raised her sword to protect herself and Prince Jeff by covering them with a shield.

Speed Twister muttered a spell and shoveled his magic pen above Mother Reddy's head; instantly, she was able to sway her paws, wings, and tail side to side. Then she flew off gracefully at high speed after flapping her huge wings. She went into an igloo, and then another.

"Phew. A minute ago, I thought Speed Twister wanted to attack us with his magic pen, however he just wanted to unfreeze Mother Reddy!" Ashley exclaimed. "I wonder what magical elements they're searching for!" she pondered while Prince Jeff merely shrugged.

In due course, he closed his eyes tightly.

"What are you doing, Prince Jeff?" Ashley enquired.

"I am gifted with magic to detect the ancient sacred items that Speed Twister is searching for by his skin touching mine. There is a limitation. Only the royal creatures from the Goodness Realm can detect it. However, it is a tough job and requires lots of energy, as well as full concentration," Prince Jeff explained.

"Speed Twister accidentally hit my arm when he was running away. I could feel that his heart is restless, and his mind is preoccupied. They are searching for two ancient items to break the curse that was befallen on his nieces, The Three Weird Sisters," Prince Jeff continued.

"Both of them are not gifted to feel the existence of the ancient elements?" Ashley asked.

"No. Due to that, Speed Twister has no choice but to fly from one country to another to find those items."

***

"Mother Reddy, we have circled and gone from one end to another of Antarctica, but there is no sign of the ancient items. Let's leave this place and travel to the next continent." Speed Twister drew breath and released it before he spoke.

As he was talking while facing Mother Reddy, Ashley's sword produced a ray of bluish laser light towards Mother Reddy's buttock feathers, lighting them up in flames.

"Please put off the flames on my buttocks!" Mother Reddy shrieked.

"Where do you think you're going, Mother Reddy and Speed Twister? Please return the Antarctic to itself; then I will put out the fire," Ashley replied.

"You fools! You will find out yourselves how to revive the Antarctic without us. This is to teach you a lesson for cursing my nieces!" Speed Twister shouted, hopping on Mother Reddy's huge left wing.

He pointed his magic pen towards Mother Reddy's buttocks to put out the flames. The flames momentarily died before reappearing.

Prince Jeff and Ashley saw Speed Twister's reaction and quickly pointed out their swords into Mother Reddy's direction to prevent both from flying. But before Ashley and Prince Jeff were able to do anything, Mother Reddy and Speed Twister flew off.

Upon seeing this, Ashley uttered:

Only the generation of true heart grant me with great strength.

Sprinkle with love, sprinkle with heart.

Please freeze Mother Reddy.

The spell worked, and Mother Reddy's big, strong wings froze within seconds.

Immediately, she could not flap her wings up or down, which caused her to tumble down and down from the blue sky. *Splat!* She fell onto an iceberg surrounded by water.

Speed Twister was sitting on her left wing when this occurred. His eyes opened widely upon seeing the changes, quickly changed his location to the centre of Mother Reddy's body covered with feathers. This was to avoid being frozen just like Mother Reddy's left wing.

At his spot, he could view the ray of magic from Ashley's sword lingering on Mother Reddy's wings.

Clenching his teeth then he hurriedly took out his magic pen from his jacket pocket and pointed his magic towards Ashley's sword's ray of magic.

Due to the pen's magic pushing harshly, the ray of magic subsequently caused Ashley to place pressure on her sword and move forward to withhold the strain.

She used her full strength to push her sword magic further forward to maintain her balance. But due to the pressure of the magic pen, Ashley felt that her sword was about to give way from fighting the magic pen. She summersaulted and rolled over to prevent his magic from hitting her and her sword.

Once she fell from the sky, she yelled, "Bracelet! Release protection shield!"

The magic pen bounced back and hit Speed Twister's hand instead. He rolled over on Mother Reddy's back, and his face fell onto the thick feathers.

Then Prince Jeff pressed the royal emblem in the middle of his belt; it released his good-hearted magic in bright lights in a straight line. The magic darted like lightning, hitting and pushing Speed Twister's magic pen away. The magic pen tumbled from Mother Reddy's body, falling down and down from the air.

"My magic pen! Come back here!"

Without thinking, he foolishly jumped down from Mother Reddy to save his magic pen, which caused him to risk his life at twenty feet high.

His face turned pale like seeing a ghost since he was suffocated with less oxygen to breathe since he was mid-air.

Mother Reddy realized what had happened and uttered a magic spell to protect Speed Twister from hurting himself.

A magic parachute appeared on Speed Twister's back, which floated him in the air.

Upon realizing that he was safe, he manoeuvred his body in the direction of the magic pen.

A few feet below from his original location, he stretched his left hands while his legs pushed his body forward.

"Gotcha. Safe and sound with me," Speed Twister whispered.

Seeing Speed Twister flying to get hold of his magic pen, Ashley raised her sword above her head and muttered a spell, then both she and Prince Jeff were both floating beside Speed Twister.

"You are not going anywhere until you return the Antarctic to its actual temperature," Prince Jeff told him firmly.

"I will reverse the spell with the conditions that you free Mother Reddy," he replied.

"I agree. The agreement is as follows: You will return 50% of the Antarctic to the temperature and surroundings before I release Mother Reddy's right-wing. Then I will release another wing once you have turned the balance 50% of Antarctic to normal," Ashley suggested, looking sternly into Speed Twister eyes.

"That is a deal, dearie. You are becoming to be more mature in your thinking," Speed Twister replied. "I need to find a secure icy rock that is higher than the water flowing from the river to undo the spell on this side of the Antarctic. Let me try."

He took out his magic pen and pointed it towards the waterfront, then shifted his magic pen to the left, then his right side. While doing so, he uttered a few spells.

At once, the area that had previously melted turned into solid ice.

Penguins, seals, and whales who were barely surviving from the melting ice and heat finally revived. Penguins started flapping their wings happily as they walked here and there with joy.

Seals made joyful sounds as they jumped into the icy water and hopping up onto icebergs.

"Sword, release Mother Reddy's left-wing from the spell," Ashley said after placing her sword in front of her face, facing Mother Reddy once the Antarctic weather returned to normal.

"Speed Twister, please ensure that 100% of Antarctic is returned to normal climate as promised," Prince Jeff reminded him while tilted his head at him.

With this, Speed Twister raised his arms high up; this time, with two of his magic pens, he circled both around while facing the watery scenery and murmuring a spell.

The reverse spell turned the Antarctic to its usual self in an instant.

As promised, Ashley defrosted Mother Reddy's right-wing upon witnessing this. The giant bird flapped her strong wings up and down excitedly.

She moved forward and flew to Speed Twister's spot; he jumped onto her right-wing. Then he twisted and turned his magic pen while his mouth moved to say a spell.

Upon seeing this, Prince Jeff immediately activated his magic belt to prevent Speed Twister from running away.

However, the spell that Speed Twister uttered was fast and able to avoid Prince Jeff's magic.

Poof.

Both disappeared into thin air.

"Where are they?" Ashley turned around and around, looking everywhere for them.

"Stop, Ashley. They are in another country now. They travel fast with the magic pen," Prince Jeff said.

Prince Jeff closed his two blue sparkling eyes firmly, but he was unable to see anything.

"Maybe my ring and auto bracelet combined with yours will help you to view their location," Ashley suggested.

"Let's try it. One, two, three." He touched Ashley's auto ring and auto bracelet simultaneously while closing his eyes. Then he said, "I can see a lady statue in green with a torch. They are in New York, USA!"

Instantly, Ashley raised her sword above her head as well as holding Prince Jeff's hand and said:

Only the generation of true heart grant me with great strength.

Sprinkle with love, sprinkle with heart

Let us be in New York - United States of America

Poof.

CHAPTER 6

"I can feel in my bones that we are close to finding the next ancient element. I can feel the presence of unrest power. I wonder if my ancestors have been here." Speed Twister talked loudly to Mother Reddy. "Mother Reddy, please park at the foot of the green lady statue in New York. I need to do some magic detector from there since from the statue my power can cover an extensive area. If we are lucky, the ancient sacred items are hidden within this statue."

Mother Reddy flew and parked nicely at the Statue of Liberty.

Speed Twister raised both of his hands, holding both magic pens high up in the sky, waving side to side. He tried to locate the power and waves of the strength of the ancient elements.

"Oh my, I don't feel it at all. It is very disappointing. Mother Reddy, please fly further upwards location on its crown. Maybe from there I can detect the frequency of the ancient element's strength."

"Look, there is a gigantic bird; no, it is a phoenix," one visitor shouted.

"No, it is a combination of phoenix and Simargh bird." One visitor pointed her fingers at Mother Reddy as she passed by. The visitor's mouth opened wide.

"Hurry, Mother Reddy. We must not allow the Earthlings to see us. I need to erase their memory of us."

Once he reached the crown, Speed Twister took out his two magical pens on top of his head. This time, he closed his eyes to imagine and feel the presence of any powerful source of ancient elements. *Sigh.* "I could not feel any magic presence," Speed Twister said sadly, his shoulder slouched.

Suddenly, a gust of strong wind appeared, pushing his grip from the magic pen. It fell from his spot at the crown of the statue.

"Mother Reddy, fly down and catch the pen!" Speed Twister shouted for help.

Even though she was required to fly fast, it was gracefully enough that her passenger did not feel any pressure changes.

Then he was impatient and fearing that he may not be able to catch the pen since the pen was almost at a gap of five feet from himself, so he jumped off her wings and stretched his arms to grab his pen; however, his pen dropped faster than him.

Mother Reddy, to his rescue, flapped her strong wings harder, which caused her to be just below Speed Twister within a few seconds.

His chest touched the thick furry feathers, followed by his arms and legs.

Without wasting any time, she pushed her feet harder while flipping her wings larger, which caused her to fly faster down towards the magic pen's direction.

At the same time, a white-feathered bird with long-wings flew at the same level as Mother Reddy.

The shimmering magical pen caught its eyes.

As it neared the pen, it opened its beak to grab it.

Upon seeing this, Speed Twister quickly uttered a magic word while his long and skinny hands managed to grab both pens before the gull ate them.

"I am the owner; please excuse us," Speed Twister said politely to the gull with his mouth curved widely.

***

Ashley and Prince Jeff had just arrived at the foot of Statue of Liberty through Ashley's magic sword when Speed Twister was in a commotion to save his magic pen.

Once he saved it, Ashley and Prince Jeff stood opposite him while he was on Mother Reddy's wing.

"Go away from me, you two rascals!" Speed Twister scolded them.

All of a sudden, he twisted his right hand with his magic pen in mid-air, and *poof*, both disappeared like wind without leaving a trace.

CHAPTER 7

"Let's not waste time chasing both of them without any clue where the exact location of the items are hidden. How about we seek the Witchery Minister's assistance to find the location of the ancient sacred items?" Ashley suggested while her sweat appeared on her brow.

"That is a brilliant suggestion. Let's go!" Prince Jeff replied smiling.

"Speed Twister is fast like lightning, and we could not catch him." Ashley relayed their journey to Witchery Minister, Bob, and Billy in a strained voice.

Ashley and Prince Jeff returned to the Goodness Realm to seek assistance from Witchery Minister, who was known for scientific invention and development of new magic in the Goodness Realm.

"It is interesting that Speed Twister is running from one country to another searching for the antidote whereas the curse can be broken by his nieces changing their hearts. They must change from being greedy and evil to good instead," the Witchery Minister explained and simultaneously wrapped his arm around his waist.

"It is not easy for someone who was born as a witch to change their heart to pure good. They have been taught for years and years to be greedy and evil," Prince Jeff added while massaging his hair.

"I agree with you on your thoughts and analogy. It is easier said than done," Ashley responded with a nod.

Witchery Minister massaged his beard and nodded in agreement.

***

"The little rascal and her prince seem to be a hindrance to Uncle's journey in his search for an antidote," Angie said. Their crystal ball showed the events that happened.

Her left index fingers came out from her side, about to release a magic ray of light through the magic crystal ball to prevent Ashley and Prince Jeff from obstructing Speed

Twister's journey. Quickly, Danielle, with her firm grip, pushed her fingers down.

"Don't you dare disrupt Uncle's plan!" she screamed. "It would be stupid to strike our magic through the crystal ball since there is no way for our magic able to penetrate the crystal ball and hit Ashley and Prince Jeff. The only witch that has the power and capability to do so is none other than Witch Z." Danielle treaded heavily and noisily with her face turned red.

"This is the reason we require Witch Z's necklace and her powerful sceptre."

"How can we help Uncle Speed Twister find the ancient elements faster? Which country must they visit next?" Cindy wondered.

"That is a good question. Why not ignite the two ancient elements from Shanghai and Kuala Lumpur? Let's force them to spill the beans," Danielle said while her eyes were looking at the ancient Chinese wristwatch and the tip of Towers One and Two of KLCC.

"One, two, three!" The three of them raised their palms facing upwards. Upon reaching mid-air above their chest, they began to flip their palms, their skinny index fingers pointing at the two items placed beside the bowl. The two items moved gradually towards the magical bowl.

Danielle, Angie, and Cindy uttered a spell, "Arbralililoath Bibibowbow."

A sudden gust of wind passed by their faces. A twirl of wind, along with small lightning, released in the bowl once.

The fierce dragon silhouette appeared, along with the lady in white.

"Why do you summon us?" both said in unison.

This time, the two ancient elements could feel the presence of the evil spell lingering amongst the three weird sisters; therefore, both were not brave enough to fight or mock them.

"We know that you have the power to let us know where the location of other two elements are."

"Since both of you are our slaves, please bow to our command and tell us!" Danielle commanded. Her, Cindy, and Angie's eyes shone in red ray lights; their hands had a sprinkle of smoke mixed with a spark of fire as though they were possessed by demons, about to shoot both magical spirits.

Seeing this, the dragon and lady, feeling fearful, said, "We both do not have the direct answer; however, we can share with you the history in order for you to determine the whereabouts of the ancient sacred elements."

"Please begin your story without delay," command Danielle while wrapped her arms around herself.

"Yes, you must, now!" Cindy responded while Angie nodded in agreement.

"One thousand years ago, in ancient China in Beijing, there lived a family who did businesses with the Europeans. Within five years, their wealth completely changed the outlook of their homes from a small hut. Then, as the businesses grew, they lived in a traditional-looking mansion. For the family to obtain their riches, the father, a business leader, stumbled upon an ancient item. It was believed that a foreigner businessman from Europe accidentally left it at a bar in the village nearby Beijing.

"The father, who was a regular customer of the Chinese bar, while he was drinking at his table, saw a small box with a gold trim design was hidden behind a wooden chair next to his table. The small box was believed to be a size like a lady's ring box with a marbles symbol printed with an expensive thread. The father opened the box and saw one marble inside was black intertwined with silver;

another marble was intertwined with blue sapphire with black, and one at the center had a blood-red background with a knife picture on it. After staring at it a few seconds, a keeper (like a genie) appeared within the box in a smoke formation. The keeper promised to make the Chinese father wealthy by turning him into the famous businessman that deals with European markets."

"Does this mean that the ancient sacred items that we are looking for are the three marbles that fit the description you both just shared with us? I make a wild guess that its location will be in Europe, but which part of Europe?" Danielle asked in an impatient tone.

The dragon spirit explained, "Yes, those marbles are what you must find. It remains a mystery where the family of the said father hid it. It was believed that his family had to flee in a ship to another country to hide against the European businessman after his tea poisoned them."

"Argh! We only know that the ancient sacred items are in Eastern Europe, and Europe is large. This will take so much time for Speed Twister and Mother Reddy to locate them," Danielle responded in despair.

Clap. Clap. Clap. They finally found the clue. Angie responded, "Next, the lady in white, please spill the beans!"

The lady in white closed her eyes and placed her skinny long fingers at the side of her forehead and said:

"I saw in my vision that the last ancient sacred items you are required to find are the ancient koala and kangaroo teeth and nails found in Australia. There is a belief that the two sacred items bring strength to those who wear them over their necks. But on the other hand, it can cause death to the beholder once the beholder becomes greedy by going against the sacred will."

"Thanks for sharing the essential information; this will make our search faster," Danielle answered.

Both the dragon and the lady in white disappeared into their two ancient elements.

Then the Three Weird Sisters released their palms, uttered a spell, and placed the two items beside the magic bowl.

***

Next, Danielle walked towards her royal chair and stopped, muttering a spell. "My magic crystal ball, please oh please tell me where Speed Twister and Mother Reddy are," Danielle said in her sweet voice.

Within a few seconds, a magic crystal ball floated in front of her eyes with smoke in grey and white colour enveloping it. The crystal ball screen blinked, and then it showed Speed Twister with his face haggard with tiredness as he walked on a sandy beach. Mother Reddy was walking beside him with her wings flapping slowly.

“Where on Earth is this beach? Is it in Malibu?” Danielle asked with furrowed brows.

Thereafter, the crystal ball gave the three weird sisters a hint on Speed Twister’s whereabouts. It showed a beach with a prominent building at the seafront, one that appeared to be made up of a ship’s sail with a helipad near the roof.

“So, Speed Twister and Mother Reddy are at Jumaira Beach Pavillion; the building is the most expensive hotel in the world located in Dubai,” Angie said, reading the information on the internet via her magic wristwatch.

“'They are wasting their time by searching for the sacred item on the beach of Dubai! We need to contact them and give them the correct direction,” Danielle said.

“How do you suggest we contact them?” Cindy asked.

“Of course, by our magic crystal ball.”

Danielle raised her arms with her palms facing the beaded ceiling decorated with a toffee crystal chandelier. As she did that, the crystal chandelier collided with each other, causing clashing sounds; then, her two hands moved in a small circle that created a transparent ball.

Then she said, "DahhlieexistDahlieexistica."

Speed Twister was holding his magic pen trying to identify any ancient sacred items hidden in the sandy beach when he felt a gust of wind that caused his hair to sway side to side, blinding his vision. Then, all of a sudden, the beach sand flew aside bit by bit; His eyes opened wider than usual, bewildered to witness that the sand was writing a message.

He exclaimed while looking at the sand, "Mother Reddy, look, there is a message."

In the sand, it said, "Speed Twister, look no further in this land;

We found the location and items you need to seek for our freedom:

A ring box with three marbles engraved on it is hidden in Eastern Europe.

Furthermore, other sacred items to find are in the form of the ancient koala and kangaroo teeth and nails believed to be hidden in Australia."

After reading aloud, the wind blew the wordings, replacing them with sand.

“Mother Reddy, my nieces found a better clue for this project. Let’s go to Australia first, as it is at the southern direction from Dubai. We must return to our realm via Europe route which will be our next stop,” Speed Twister said as he jumped onto Mother Reddy’s left-wing.

Both disappeared in thin air after walking at the Jumaira’s beach.

CHAPTER 8

Speed Twister and Mother Reddy finally arrived in Sydney, Australia.

"Mother Reddy." Speed Twister inhaled deeply. "I can smell the fresh air. Look, we can see the Sydney Opera House from here. It is the famous building among tourists and their residents. The structure resembles three clamshells interlocking with each other."

"Fly forward, Mother Reddy, and land on the roof. From the top, I will be able to detect any power." Speed Twister pointed with his fingers.

Once Mother Reddy landed, Speed Twister started to stand on Mother Reddy's wing, as he was excited to feel the strength of the ancient sacred power.

He breathed in and out while stretching his hands to feel for any power.

"I don't feel anything, Mother Reddy. Let me check another round."

"Magic pen, magic pen, do your wonders." He circled both of his hands, holding the magic pen to feel the ancient sacred power while standing, and closed his eyes with the hope that he could see any silhouette of the sacred items.

Nothing happened. Breathing deeply, Speed Twister uttered again, "Please detect the ancient sacred elements." He circled both his arms anti-clockwise this time while holding magic pens in both hands.

Suddenly, they felt and saw a gust of wind with flickering lights in green colour gliding through the clouds that pushed Speed Twister back from the spot he was standing.

The strong force made him roll backward, leaving behind Mother Reddy. Sydney's harbor was gradually covered with snow.

"Why the weather change? It is supposed to be summer," a passer-by shouted aloud while he hugged himself and shivered in the cold. He was wearing a t-shirt and Bermuda shorts.

"Oh my, did my magic pen turn Sydney's weather to winter?" Speed Twister wondered while twisting his moustache with one of his fingers.

***

In the Goodness Realm, the rectangular shape of a box suddenly appeared from the corner of a cupboard. It began to blink to get attention.

It showed light snow falling from the sky of Sydney during summer.

"Oh, no! Not again. This must be the work of Speed Twister. Sydney has turned into the ice-like Antarctic during the summer season!" Prince Jeff exclaimed while shaking his fist.

"Looks like we have to save Sydney," Ashley and Bob chorused at the same time.

Ashley raised her sword above her head as well as holding Prince Jeff's hand and uttered:

Only the generation of true heart grant me with great strength.

Sprinkle with love, sprinkle with heart.

Let us be in Sydney, Australia.

Poof.

Ashley, Prince Jeff, and Bob appeared standing on the pavement entrance of the Sydney Opera house.

"Bob, you followed us?" Ashley asked.

"I want to help you, Ashley; that is the reason I held onto your sweater when you said the spell," Bob replied.

Those around them hunched down, shielding themselves from the cold. Some trembled in fear and cold while biting their fingernails. Others wrapped their arms around themselves, puzzled by the latest development of the sudden weather change.

"Where can Speed Twister and Mother Reddy be looking for the ancient element?" Ashley whispered to Prince Jeff and Bob.

***

"Featherdale Sydney Wildlife Park, here we come." Speed Twister was all smiles, thinking they would finally get the third ancient sacred element.

Mother Reddy flew into the wildlife park at the center of the entrance, which was full of greenery and well-trimmed grass. Her big, strong wings flapped up and down when she landed, creating a stir of commotion for the wildlife. Upon landing, she leaned against some bushes, causing it to remove from its roots and roll on the driveway.

"What are you, and why are you here?" a female attendant in a green shirt holding a baby koala asked.

"Hi there, I am the famous Speed Twister. I am the leader of the Maze Realm, and I am here to search for the ancient sacred koala and kangaroo teeth and nails I believe must be hiding in your zoo. And who are you?" Speed Twister asked.

"I am Beth, the warden for this wildlife park. What can I do for you?" she answered.

As he twisted his fingers staring at Beth, suddenly she was under his spell. Her body and eyes froze like a robot.

The other people and animals turned to copper covered with thick white snow, unable to move a muscle, faces stiff like statues.

"You are now under my command, Beth. This will do the trick and buy some time for me to search for the ancient sacred items," Speed Twister whispered to Mother Reddy. "Since you are huge, please stay here. If anything mysterious happens, please be on guard and be a warrior," he said to Mother Reddy. Then he turned to the attendant. "Beth, show me the oldest koalas and kangaroos that you have. Also, any preserved dead koalas and kangaroos."

Being under Speed Twister's magic spell, Beth started marching like sleep walking as her eyes and head remained fixed forward.

After lots of bends and curved routes that both had to take to reach a deserted room, they finally got a room with signage indicated as STAFF ENTRANCE.

***

Upon entering the room, there was a frozen middle-aged man with a classic side-part hairstyle with chin stubble sitting on a stool with his hands holding a small carving knife; there was an aged koala frozen in front of him.

"This is the preparation for ancient Australian exhibits scheduled to open to public within two months," Beth explained. "Follow me to the preservation room located at the back; this is where we keep the majority of ancient koalas, kangaroos, wombats, and others for the exhibit events."

Speed Twister was all smiles upon hearing his good fortune.

Once they both reached the preservation room, Beth unlocked the door and guided Speed Twister inside.

"You may look around and take the only two items as you wish."

Speed Twister raised his both arms while holding two of his magic pens; he twisted and turned his wrists, which caused some wind to appear, and then he sprinkled some magic dust here and there in the room. All of sudden, an ancient skeleton koala began walking towards him.

It caught Speed Twister's eye, making him curl his fingers tightly and wave for the ancient koala to approach him.

Once he stood a few feet away from Speed Twister, the koala extended his paw to show Speed Twister his old black nails.

At a glance, it looked like an ordinary nail; however, as Speed Twister stared at it for a minute, there was a shape of a tiny crescent embedded in it.

"That is the ancient sacred items that I need. Kindly share with me." Speed Twister pointed with his fingers at the koala's index nail.

The magic powder and magic pen caused him to be under his spell; therefore, the ancient koala willingly pulled its index fingernails without any tingling or numbness feelings.

"Thank you, and what about your ancient teeth? Please open your mouth and show me."

The koala shook its head to inform Speed Twister that there were none. The koala opened his mouth widely, however, only uneven gums remained.

"None," Speed Twister groaned in misery.

Next was Mr. Kangaroo's turn. "Mr. Kangaroo, where are you?" Speed Twister shoved his magic pen on the ceiling and said, "From my power I can feel your presence, Mr. Kangaroo, you are hidden in the three-tiered cabinet on my left side. Please show yourself," he called out.

An old kangaroo with bushy white eyebrows and droopy ears hopped from the side of the cabinet to the center near to the worktable; then, it slowly hopped further nearer to the spot Speed Twister was standing.

"Show me your teeth and nails."

The kangaroo obediently opened his mouth; instantly, a shining tooth in thick silver gleamed in Speed Twister's eyes, which blinded him.

He felt that it would be difficult and painful for the kangaroo to remove said teeth, so Speed Twister took out one of his magic pens and said a spell to remove the teeth. Lucky for the kangaroo, due to the magic pen, the process of pulling its teeth was a painless experience.

"Next, please show me your fingernails."

Again, the kangaroo moved its right and left hands to face Speed Twister without any hesitation.

"Let me see, one, two, three, four, five. Nothing seems peculiar on the right hand. Next hand, please. Hm, looks like an ordinary finger. Let me double-check."

He started tapping all the ten fingernails with his magic pen, but all the ten fingernails had nothing.

"Thank you. Both kangaroo and koala, you may return to your place now; I have found two items to assist with my nieces' freedom. However, I am required to find another two items to complete the sacred items from Australia."

Then he pushed the door to return to the entrance; someone had locked the door.

"Beth! Beth! Please unlock this door."

Speed Twister quickly uttered a spell to open the door.

Then he felt a slight shudder of the door. The door flung open with Beth standing stoutly in front.

"Move aside, Beth! Where is another location for finding the ancient koala teeth and kangaroo fingernails?"

Beth was still under Speed Twister's spell and could not speak normally; however, she whispered so softly that only Speed Twister could hear it.

In a flash, he ran like a bullet train, passing by the wildlife sanctuary before arriving to the entrance. His spell vanished in the air once he arrived the entrance, leaving Beth turning into her normal self, which led her feeling appalled, not understanding why she was standing in front of the STAFF ENTRANCE room.

"Mother Reddy, off we go to the Melbourne Museum!"

Her enormous strong wings, enveloped with feathers, started to flap up and down ferociously just as Ashley, Prince Jeff, and Bob arrived.

"Stop!" Prince Jeff immediately released his magic power from his royal belt towards Speed Twister. In contrast, Ashley's auto bracelet cast two nets that fell onto Mother Reddy to prevent her from flying. Her wings struggled to break free by flapping; however, the net's grip was strong that prevented them from moving.

The magic ray of lights released by Prince Jeff's belt was not strong enough to hit Speed Twister at his spot.

"Rerelilitemore. Rerelilitemore!" Speed Twister shouted, raising one of his magic pens with the sacred teeth and nails facing both of Mother Reddy's wings.

In the blink of an eye, the net disappeared, releasing Mother Reddy's wing; she rigorously flapped her wings as fast as she could while her feet pushed from the ground.

Seeing this, Ashley and Prince Jeff stood still at their position while their lips closed together.

Prince Jeff's face turned to dismay with lines visible on his forehead. "Guess the ancient sacred item from Sydney that Speed Twister found is stronger than our magic."

CHAPTER 9

At the Melbourne Museum, Speed Twister noticed that several security cameras were installed and surrounded the locked museum door, which was made from thick solid wood.

"Amazing how these humans think so little of the magic," Speed Twister said, smiling. "AjaAjarelili, AjaAjarelili."

Speed Twister twisted and turned his wrists while holding two magic pens, and then the door opened widely and silently. Then he pointed his magic pens to deactivate the security camera and alarm.

With another spell, Mother Reddy became the size of his palm.

"I cannot let Ashley and her prince see you. Both will know I am here if they do." He looked at Mother Reddy.

Once they opened the entrance door of the museum and entered, the first item that they saw was the directory listing. The directory encompassed three levels of rooms.

Underneath the directory was a statue of koala and kangaroos made of copper. A few feet from it was the three-tiered staircase.

From the list, the koala museum section caught his eye. The location was on the second floor on the left.

Since he was born with speed, Speed Twister ran fast like lightning through the convex-shaped staircases. Soon, he reached the koala exhibition section. Subsequently, he took his magic pens, made a little twist of his hands, and pointed at the door; it sprang open. Inside, the room was in pitch-black darkness.

Speed Twister threw a speck of magic dust above the koala exhibition section. "Show me the way." Then the magic dust developed into an arrow to indicate the way to find the ancient sacred element.

He walked to the main exhibit room while Mother Reddy flew by his side. Upon reaching the room, the magic arrow pointed to the right towards another room. After walking a few steps, the magic arrow remained floating facing a smaller room.

Then Speed Twister pushed the door open. The first item he saw was a transparent glass museum showcase located at the centre of the room. His mouth opened widel,y then it curved moving upwards.

It was decorated with shining crystal, guarded by two long braveheart axes that were placed on both sides of the showcase.

Curious, both went nearer the showcase; there was a koala with its mouth open widely on the other side. In it, two teeth were shining, one in gold and another in silver.

"AjaAjarelili, AjaAjarelili!"

Speed Twister twisted and turned his wrists while holding two magic pens, which raised the showcase. Suddenly, the alarm detector triggered, which released several blaring short sounds. Speed Twister froze upon hearing the noise, his eyes widening. Mother Reddy gave him a nudge; he recovered from the shock and quickly cast a spell on the alarm detector. His magic paralyzed the alarm.

"Sigh," Speed Twister whispered to Mother Reddy. "I nearly got my first heart attack."

His heartbeat was faster than usual. *Maybe my creeping existence in the museum has disabled the security alarm*, he thought.

Without wasting any time, at top speed, his arms squeezed into the tiny space of the showcase to grab the two sacred elements.

While Speed Twister ran to the second floor and walked into the koala exhibit, Ashley and Prince Jeff had just reached the museum entrance with the assistance of Ashley's magic sword.

Prince Jeff was born to be able to detect the whereabouts of creatures by touching their skin, which he did with Speed Twister in the Antarctic. Thus, he was able to determine Speed Twister was here.

"Stop!" Prince Jeff said with his sword pointing in Speed Twister's direction.

Ashley's sword released a ray of bluish light, hitting Speed Twister's hands, burning them, which made him release his grip on both items.

They dropped and rolled on the epoxy-coated flooring.

Speed Twister clenched his jaw and shouted, "You little rascals! I need those items!"

At lightning speed, he ran and then tumbled on the floor, extending his long, skinny hands.

"Got it!" He bared his white teeth.

He quickly uttered a spell while twisting and twirling his two hands.

Poof.

He was gone. He was too fast for Ashley.

***

Next, Speed Twister ran fast as lightning to the level 3 east wing in search for the kangaroo's nail. He recalled from the directory that he read upon entering the musuem that the kangaroo exhibit was here.

He made sure to look all around him, just in case Ashley and Prince Jeff showed up.

"AjaAjarelili, AjaAjarelili!"

Speed Twister twisted and turned his wrists while holding two magic pens. The door to the kangaroo exhibit opened just enough to allow him to enter with Mother Reddy.

Luck was with him; the kangaroo nails he was searching for were located a few mere feet from where he stood. A large preserved kangaroo was displayed in the center of the wooden floor.

Upon reaching the preserved kangaroo, Speed Twister saw that its nails were not visible. His face turned pale.

All of a sudden, a silhouette of Ashley appeared beside the preserved kangaroo, and then she came out from hiding behind it. Both stood a few feet opposite each other.

"Looking for this?" Ashley pointed a kangaroo nail in shining gold with a smile and one arm folded on her side waist.

Speed Twister's blue face turned to red cherry with some smoke fuming from his hair in a shaped of smashed meatballs. "Give that to me. That is mine, you little rascals!"

He instantly took out his magic pen and released a red ray of light in Ashley's direction.

Ashley quickly reacted to avoid the laser beam of his magic. "Ring, release a shield against fire."

In an instant, a shield in the shape of a half circle made from aramid fiber and Kevlar materials that could withstand heat covered Ashley and Prince Jeff. It prevented the red ray of light from hitting them.

"Please, stop! Speed Twister, let us discuss this like gentlemen," Ashley pleaded.

"We will give you the sacred kangaroo nail on one condition; you will return Sydney to its normal season and temperature!" Prince Jeff shouted while standing opposite Speed Twister.

"That is a good deal. I will change the climate immediately. Please follow me to witness the change," Speed Twister responded.

Like wildfire, Speed Twister and Mother Reddy appeared in front of the museum entrance.

Ashley and Prince Jeff followed them to witness their action.

Standing at the top of the Sydney opera house roof, Speed Twister took out his magic pen, pointing at the vast water areas in front, middle, and then his right side; while doing so, he uttered a few spells.

The climate changed bit by bit to summer.

"This is the sacred nail in exchange." Ashley placed it on his palm.

"By the way, it is cumbersome for you to go from country to country to find the antidote to the spell. So, the only way to break my spell is for the Three Weird Sisters to change their hearts and attitudes to be good." Ashley begged.

He nodded and replied, "It is impossible for evil witches that were born evil and had ancestors that were greedy and evil for centuries to change to be good immediately."

Mother Reddy returned to her enormous size, her huge, feathered wings flapping fast up and down.

"Where is your next destination? We can help you locate the final ancient sacred elements," Ashley said upon seeing Mother Readdy preparing to fly. She raised her right hand with palm out.

Both ignored Ashley's question. Mother Reddy flew away with Speed Twister sitting safely on her.

Speed Twister elevated his chin, held his head high, twisted and turned his magic pens in both hands. His mouth muttered a spell and …

Poof.

Both were gone in the blink of an eye.

"Not to worry, Ashley, I managed to pluck one of Mother Reddy's feathers when she changed herself to a larger bird. With her feathers, my magical technology sword will be able to detect their whereabouts in an instant," Prince Jeff said with a smile.

He raised his royal sword high up above his head and threw Mother Reddy's feather towards the blade. Instantaneously, smoke in light blue appeared above his forehead.

The silhouette of Mother Reddy appeared within the smoke; it displayed her flying, flapping her wings slowly, and descending on a gondola surrounded by dirty water.

CHAPTER 10

Ashley raised her sword above her head, as well as holding Prince Jeff's hand, while Bob clutched her feet, and said:

Only the generation of true heart grant me with great strength.

Sprinkle with love, sprinkle with heart

Let us be in Venice, Italy.

Poof.

Tourists and shoppers were looking at Ashley and Prince Jeff's costume, their eyes moving from head to toe. Ashley's face was adorned with a pink filigree mask with rhinestones, resembling a Venetian mask during the Venice carnival.

It was weird for anyone to dress up in a masked costume in broad daylight; therefore, locals looked astonished. They walked to the stacio of the canal to search for Speed Twister and Mother Reddy.

Within a few minutes, when they could not locate them after walking from one stacio to another, Prince Jeff again released his sword from above his head with Mother Reddy's feather thrown above it.

A puff of magic smoke cropped up in front of Prince Jeff showed him the silhouette of two of Mother Reddy's wings struggling to fly away. Her wings were pulled back down by a steel wired rope, and a twisted rope tied her beak tightly.

"Did you see that? Is she being captured, or is she stuck?" Prince Jeff asked Ashley and Bob.

"Maybe you can view the location of Speed Twister in order for us to determine whether Mother Reddy is in trouble?" Ashley suggested.

"You are right, Ashley." Prince Jeff shovelled his sword and threw Mother Reddy's feather above his blade again. This time, a puff of smoke appeared with blurry images of Speed Twister, and then a few seconds later, once the smoke dispersed, it showed Speed Twister. This time his size was small, like a pen, and he was kept in a cage made of steel with electric fencing.

"Oh my! Even his mouth is gagged with tape to prevent him from uttering any magical spells. We must save them!" Ashley exclaimed.

"Sword, please show us their location," Prince Jeff said.

Then it displayed a small café with signage, "Venice Haven." Magical smoke emitted from Prince Jeff's sword and showed Speed Twister's whereabouts. The café Venice Haven was located across Grand Canal of San Marco, the southeast district at Dorsoduro.

Ashley raised her sword above her head and muttered a spell:

Only the generation of true heart grant me with great strength.

Sprinkle with love, sprinkle with heart.

Transport us to café Venice Haven.

Poof.

Out of the blue, they appeared in front of the café; it was past the opening hours, so the cafe was covered in darkness. They could see wooden chairs were stacked in front of the restaurant, ready to welcome their customers the next day.

When Ashley, Prince Jeff, and Bob arrived, they wore masks resembling the Venetian masks during the Venice carnival in order to blend in the crowds. But since there was no current carnival, Ashley turned her outlook to her ordinary blue dress, and without wearing any mask, she looked like a typical young teenager.

"Let's check out the back of the café; I have a hunch that Speed Twister and Mother Reddy may be captured and hidden there," Ashley suggested.

Prince Jeff and Bob nodded in response.

While they approached the back of the café, they saw a dim light enlighten a small house opposite the back of the café. The three of them crept as quietly as they could to prevent the owner from hearing their footsteps and destroying their plan to save Mother Reddy and Speed Twister.

Crack!

Prince Jeff accidentally stepped on a wooden branch with his heavy leather shoe. The noise made them stop momentarily out of caution. Prince Jeff's heart skipped a beat while Ashley's shoulder stiffened.

They turned their heads to the left, center, and right side, fearing an appearance of the owners.

"Phew!" Prince Jeff sighed.

Upon reaching the back of the café, they found a tiny house. Ashley and Prince Jeff peeped into a cracked window located a few steps from the tiny house's entrance.

The tiny house was filled with haystacks piled up at the corner on the right side. There was one worn rocking chair set in front of the neatly piled haystack with a small barrel. A long wooden working table was placed next to the barrel. The table had piles of books on its corner left with some writing appliances in the middle of the table. Next, at the right side of the long table was a Bunsen burner with a purple liquid boiling.

Both noticed another two-story house made from bricks believed to be the main house of both owners.

Then they heard a whistling song emerged from the small house. Both peered inside the same window and saw the bulky body of a man with folded sleeves and a pen placed on his right ear suddenly appear at the working table.

He was uttering some spells, throwing different colours and shapes of stones into a bowl then pouring the mixture into the Bunsen. Then a colourful smoke emerged from the bowl, making the bulky man's face red. He started coughing.

Prince Jeff exchanged signals with Ashley, indicating that the man had stones made from weak magic.

"Argh, Speed Twister, hand me your magic pen. I need your magic to revive my café's glory. We need to create a delicious menu," the man sneered, facing towards a cage surrounded by barbed wire.

The man opened the cage door, grabbed Speed Twister in upside down direction then placed him into a bowl mixed with chemicals, as he was about to utter a spell.

Bob meowed in pain when he accidentally ran into a bucket full of nails. He tried to distract the bulky man so Ashley and Prince Jeff would be able to initiate their escape plans.

"Who is that?" the man called out. He returned Speed Twister into the cage and locked it. "I will get you after this," he whispered.

Ashley and Prince Jeff remained still like logs, holding their breaths to prevent any form of movement.

The door sprang open widely, the bulky man now eye to eye with Bob.

"Meow … meow."

"Oh, it's you, clumsy cat; you must have hurt yourself. Let Papa clean you." The shop owner took Bob in his arms and gently patted his fur.

Ashley and Prince Jeff came out from their hiding place; both remained in a crouching position, inching their way bit by bit to ensure the owner did not spot them both. Once they reached the cracked window, Ashley's finger that wore the auto ring shone towards the glass. The green ray of light pushed the window swiftly. Both of them jumped through the window into the small house and rolled on the floor, as the window was a few feet high.

When both entered the house, both hid at the back of the piled haystack. From their spot, they could see that the door was left ajar as the the bulky guy walked to his house opposite this small work hut. "My darling, you found a cat; his fur is beautiful," the café owner's wife said to her husband while standing in front of her house entrance.

"Let's wash its wound and place some ointment on it for it to recover, and then we have to let it go," the bulky man said in a comforting voice. While he was busy focusing on Bob, Ashley and Prince Jeff took this opportunity to save Speed Twister.

Once they were inside the work hut, Ashley and Prince Jeff walked swiftly towards the wooden worktable.

Then they both searched for the cage. In addition, they checked underneath the table just in case the bulky man hid it on the floor.

"Weird. I'm positive that the man placed the cage on the table before Bob distracted him," Ashley said in a puzzled tone.

Without wasting any time, Ashley Sprinkler activated her auto bracelet to detect any movements.

Within a few seconds, the auto bracelet emitted an apple green light in a straight line direction, facing the edge of the table.

"Let's heed the signal," Prince Jeff suggested.

Once they reached the end of the apple green light, both noticed that there was a hidden secret door latch just beside the worktable. The latch was bolted with a brass lock.

Ashley turned her head, overlooking the table. A few feet away from the table was a wooden wall; however, it was bare, and there was no key visible within reach.

Prince Jeff pointed his fingers towards Ashley's auto ring on her finger as a signal for her to use it to assist in breaking the brass lock.

Ashley pointed her auto ring towards the direction of the latch, and a ray of green light emerged. It burnt the latch. In an instant, this action caused the wooden door to slide aside, releasing a hole with a birdcage placed on a wooden flooring.

"Wait, Ashley, do not touch the items; I can feel the presence of an electronic current protecting the cage. This can burn your hands." Prince Jeff waved at Ashley to stop. Then, he placed a pen onto the cage wires, and the cell released smoke, which eventually turned into black ashes.

Upon witnessing this, Ashley shoved her sword into the cage's direction, freeing the cage from the electronic current; once it died, Prince Jeff released the ray of light from his royal belt to open the latch of the cage door.

Ashley quickly picked up Speed Twister with her auto bracelet power and placed him into her pocket.

“Next is to save Mother Reddy and Bob. Where is she hiding?” Ashley whispered to Speed Twister, pulling him towards her ear to hear him speaking.

“She is placed at the front of the café as a decoration to attract customers.” he whispered shakily.

Ashley and Prince Jeff gasped.

Hastily, Ashley uttered, “Auto bracelet, shut the cage.”

Instantly, the door and latch were closed tightly. This action was to prevent any suspicion as Speed Twister escaped.

Then, they could hear heavy footsteps approaching the work hut; all three of their hearts beat faster while the hair on their hands stood still; quick-thinking, Ashley uttered a spell while raising her sword. Then Ashley, Prince Jeff, and Speed Twister appeared in front of the café verandah.

They saw Mother Reddy struggling with her wings moving left and right, trying to break free from the steel chain, her head moving restlessly due to the tightness of the rope.

"Auto ring, release this chain," Ashley commanded. A ray of green light emerged and hit the steel chain on Mother Reddy's wing; it was like laser cutting the chain into halves. Again, her enormous, strong wings started to flap up and down, this time slowly, in order to not wake the owners. Then the auto ring cut the twisted rope that tied her beak. She opened and closed her beak without making any sound.

A door hinge sprang open; hearing this made Ashley and Prince Jeff quickly drop to a crouching position, Prince Jeff started to swallow constantly while hiding behind Mother Reddy's body.

"You good for nothing cat, scratching my wife's hands and legs until they bleed. Out you go!" the bulky man shouted at Bob while grabbing a broom that was lying against the corner of the entrance door.

Bob ran for his life. He went straight to the front of the café instead of hiding elsewhere. "Bob, we are here; come quickly," Ashley whispered, cupped her hands at the side of her mouth.

Bob, having sharp hearing, heard her whisper. He smiled to himself and ran straight to the spot where Ashley and Prince Jeff were hiding.

Ashley grabbed hold of Speed Twister from her dress pocket and whispered, "You have the magic back in Maze Realm to turn yourself to your original size, so let's go there. I will assist in transporting you and Mother Reddy to be placed in Maze Realm immediately. I am worried sick that the the bulky man's spell may be permanent if not treated fast."

After cursing Bob, the bulky man immediately returned to his work hut. He proceeded with his initial plan of getting Speed Twister out from the cage to get a hold of his magic pen and complete his delicious food spell.

He sat on a chair at his working table, looking at the boiling chemicals in the Bunsen, and then he turned himself to the right to grab Speed Twister. As he opened the latch of the door, his mouth fell open, and his face turned red. His hands were trembling with rage. "Where is Speed Twister? I am sure I caught and locked him safely here!" Instantly, he got up from his working chair, and the chair fell to the floor.

"Intruders! Intruders! Could you give me back my possession?"

Hearing his loud, shrieking voice and seeing his shadow approaching the café verandah, Ashley raised her sword above her head. She simultaneously held Prince Jeff's hand, who was seated on Mother Reddy's feathers, with Bob clutching Ashley's feet.

She uttered a spell:

Only the generation of true heart grant me with great strength.

Sprinkle with love, sprinkle with heart.

Transport all five of us to Maze Realm.

CHAPTER 11

Upon reaching the Maze Realm, Maiden of Maze appeared in a stunning velvet orange dress with lace trimmings on her neck standing at the realm's entrance.

"My, oh my, look who is here. My sweet child Ashley, you look grown-up," Maiden said with a smile.

"Hi, Maiden, it's good to see you again. I am here to find an antidote to an Italian spell placed upon Speed Twister." Ashley took Speed Twister from her pocket. Maiden's eyes widened, and her mouth curved downwards into a frown.

"My, oh my, Speed Twister is under an Italian spell."

"Maiden, dear, I lost my magic pen while trying to break free from the spell battling for my life with the bulky Italian man. My pens were mixed in his Bunsen spell that turned me to this size! What a disrespectful old man!" Speed Twister shouted with his face turned red like a tomato.

"We need to disperse the spell immediately since an Italian spell can ruin and destroy us creatures from the Maze Realm. It is known through our traditional family history."

Maiden Lady of the Maze Realm used her magic scepter to place Speed Twister in the magic study room located at the realm's edge.

She explained, "Ashley and Prince Jeff, I require your assistance in reviving Speed Twister since I remembered the book of spells; the only way to beat the Italian spell is that we require two spells from outside the Maze Realm."

"Sure, we are here to help. Please inform us what spell is required for us to revive and undo the spell," Prince Jeff said.

"With the count of one, two, three, four, five—Ashley, please use your magical sword while saying any reverse spell. As for you, Your Highness, please use the magic from your royal belt," Maiden Lady of the Maze Realm suggested.

Both placed Speed Twister at the center of the magic study room encircled by Maiden Lady of Maze Realm, Ashley Sprinkler, and Prince Jeff. All three used their magical elements, i.e., the Maze scepter, Ashley's sword of true heart, and Prince Jeff's magical royal belt. All the elements activated simultaneously to release a ray of orange, blue, and greenish lights above Speed Twister's head.

Bit by bit, Speed Twister's size changed from the size of an ant to an iguana; then, as he was about to stand tall as the same height and weight as before, all of a sudden, they felt a gust of strong wind in the study room. The current pushed stronger at Ashley's sword, causing her to lose her grip. Then the wind blew at Ashley's body, causing her to topple and fall down on the floor. Her sword fell onto the ground a few feet away from her. As she got up and grabbed hold of her sword, magical light in red appeared, burning her hands.

"What on Earth is happening?" Prince Jeff and Ashley exclaimed simultaneously.

"Ha ha ha! The sacred escape information is a win-win situation, Speed Twister. Speed Twister made a promise in an exchange for information. I gave him information on the location of ancient sacred items in Shanghai and Kuala Lumpur. In return, Speed Twister is to help me escape. Thank you for bringing Professor Sprinkler's sword and his daughter. I am lucky to have two of them from the inheritance of Professor Sprinkler." The man on a horse in the painting talked.

Ashley, Prince Jeff, and the Maiden's eyes opened widely, looking at the direction of a painting with a man on a horse in a garden full of lush greenery. All three of them blinked their eyes when the man in the picture got down from his horse and stood to face them.

"Stop looking at me as though I am a ghost. I was placed here by none other than your wicked heartless father, Professor Sprinkler."

"Father would only lock up wicked men, so what unholy activities did you do?" Ashley asked, scowling.

She was trying to distract the magical spirit's attention to grab hold of her sword. Therefore, she was asking questions that may trigger a sense of irritation so that the magical spirit grew angry.

"It is not an unholy act, little girl; it was a madness of power that I loath for my life! It happened one hundred years ago, when I was the most sought-after scientist in the whole realm." The spirit threw a hostile glare.

Before he could finish his history, Ashley swayed her sword in his direction and froze the magical spirit.

"I hope I am not too harsh in my actions. However, I am confident that my father has reasons to place him in a painting," Ashley explained to the others.

"Good of you, Ashley, on your swift thinking and action," Prince Jeff said.

"Come on; we don't have much time to save Speed Twister and change him to his original size. Otherwise, he will be banished as an ant size forever." Maiden of Maze Realm tapped her feet and repeatedly rubbed her face.

All three gathered again to encircle Speed Twister; all pointed their magical elements in Speed Twister's direction; within a few minutes, Speed Twister changed back to his normal full size.

"Oh my! Oh my! Am I back to my size?" Speed Twister exclaimed while he touched his body; then, he jumped to the end of the magic study room to check himself in the mirror, then smoothed his jacket and responded, "Yes, I am back for good." He smiled.

Then he walked nearer to Ashley and Prince Jeff while touching the tip of his moustache. He leaned against an antique writing table opposite them, standing with crossed legs.

"So, tell me, Ashley, why did you persistently want to save Mother Reddy and me back then in Venice? We have been wicked to you and Prince Jeff."

"It is the nature of a truly good heart to save a 'being' or creatures if they are in trouble because we believe that in your small, wicked heart there is goodness. Someday, you will change to a good-hearted creature," Ashley replied with a grin.

Mother Reddy, looking strained, hurriedly entered through the magic door that was able to adjust to her size. She flapped her strong wings as she entered the room.

Seeing everyone gathered at the centre with Speed Twister leaning against the bulky worktable, she quickly grabbed him with her beak.

"Oh my, Mother Reddy, why are you in a hurry?" Speed Twister cried out, kicking his legs in the air. Mother Reddy was trying her best to safely swing Speed Twister from the ground to her wing. She shrieked and then flew off.

She told him, "We have three more sacred items to gather to release your nieces from the curse. Let's not waste time."

"Wait! Let's do this together," Prince Jeff cried with his hands showing a stop signal. But unfortunately, his scream was ignored by Speed Twister and Mother Reddy.

CHAPTER 12

At the bulky table at the Maze Realm magic study room where Maiden, Ashley, and Prince Jeff were standing, Maiden shook her sceptre while muttering a spell; then, a smoke existed before her eyes. Within seconds, the Three Weird Sisters' face became clearer.

"Unbelievable, Mother Reddy is uncontrollable once she is out from Desperate Valley Realm. You should place a detector on her legs to prevent her from wandering freely," Maiden of Maze Realms reported to the Three Weird Sisters using her sceptre.

"Don't worry, Aunt Maiden, our spell covers it. Why, what happened?" Danielle asked, furrowing her brows.

Maiden related the incidents to them.

"So, I see naughty Ashley and her boyfriend are at Maze Realm. Please release this curse that your sword placed on us; we promise to be good girls," Danielle, Angie, and Cindy pleaded while bowing down on the floor to show respect.

"I wish I could disperse the curse. However, the curse will undo if you do good within the realms' community thoroughly deep in your heart," Ashley replied in a sad voice.

Hearing this, Danielle turned red from her ears to her face; her fingers were shaking. Then Danielle, Angie, and Cindy stood up with their eyes burning with anger, their palms facing their magic crystal ball.

"Ashley, run for your life!" Prince Jeff shouted at her. He grabbed her waist and pulled her aside. Then, he dragged his royal cape to cover Ashley and himself to prevent any magic sparks from hitting them.

Maiden, blinking her eyes and realizing that the Three Weird Sisters were extremely angry, quickly said a spell and removed her magic spectre from any form of communication with the Three Weird Sisters.

It was in the nick of a time; this action was able to prevent any form of magic from the Three Weird Sisters from passing through the crystal ball hitting Maiden of the Maze Realm and Ashley.

Due to misconnection at Maiden's side, the Three Weird Sisters' magic went through the crystal ball halfway and bounced back.

This reaction caused retaliation of magic power that clashed with the magic crystal ball. It quivered, and then glass flew towards the Three Weird Sisters.

"Argh! Argh!" Danielle stomped her feet on the marble floor hard.

"This will be a decade of bad luck," Angie replied in dismay, looking at the broken pieces of their magic crystal ball.

Ashley and Prince Jeff got up from their hiding place and thanked Maiden of the Maze Realm for her quick action.

"We better run along to track down Speedy Twister and Mother Reddy just in case they require us to find the last ancient sacred elements," Ashley said before she uttered with her sword above her heads:

Only the generation of true heart grant me with great strength.

Sprinkle with love, sprinkle with heart.

Please transport us to Mother Reddy and Speed Twister's whereabouts.

Poof.

CHAPTER 13

Speed Twister noticed that Mother Reddy was reducing her speed from travelling from the Maze Realm to Earth. Upon seeing a long land surrounded by three seas, Speed Twister felt goosebumps creeping on his blue skin.

"Whatever you do, we must never return to Venice. This time, we would be positively a lump of dead meat if we bumped into those evil Italians from that cafe. So, tell me, where are you bringing me?" Speed Twister asked Mother Reddy.

"Good thinking, Mother Reddy." He clapped simultaneously, his mouth curving to the side. "Rome, the holy city, the sacred item may be buried or kept hidden there. But then there are multiple places in Rome that the ancient sacred items can be hiding; can it be in the Colosseum, or in one of the churches, Sistine Chapel or

Basilica, or maybe at the bottom of the Trevi Fountain?" Speed Twister started to massage the tip of his moustache while thinking of the possibility.

Back in the Desperate Valley Realm, the ends of the Three Weird Sisters' hair burnt when their magic crystal ball went berserk; it exploded and smashed itself.

With some of their faces covered with burnt smoke, Danielle sighed, "Now we do not have any crystal ball to track Uncle's whereabouts."

"Not to worry, Danielle, we have another see-through crystal in a different shape; it is our good old magic crystal photo frame." Angie smiled and wriggled her right hand to release the crystal photo frame. The object was covered with shimmering dust.

"This looks new. Will it work as efficiently as the crystal ball?" Danielle asked while her finger touched her chin, thinking.

"*Crystal frame, crystal of Desperate Valley,*

Show me the location of Speed Twister," Angie commanded.

The frame tilted slightly aside but remained blank.

"Crystal frame of life,

Crystal frame of evil,

Show me what you've got." Danielle muttered the spell after her sister Angie's spell did not work. Then she raised her ten skinny fingers, facing the crystal frame.

Next, a ray of red lights came from her eye's direction into the crystal frame.

The frame was engulfed with smoke and stardust dancing around it, and then Speed Twister's face appeared in the center; he appeared to be lost in his thoughts.

"Look, our magic frame is showing us Speed Twister. Where is he?" Angie navigated the crystal frame to move its center inwards; there was a fountain at the background.

"He is in Rome by the Trevi Fountain!" Cindy exclaimed excitedly.

"Where do you think the ancient sacred items that are hidden in Rome? We know Rome is large," Danielle said, concentrating on the frame.

"Sisters, let's gather around and hold hands, close our eyes, and visualize that we are in Rome now," Angie suggested.

"Magic marbles, marbles of glory, show us your location."

The crystal frame returned to a blank sheet.

"Argh! Why can't our magic detect those ancient sacred items?" Cindy huffed angrily.

***

"Let's combine my ring and auto bracelet with your artifacts to view Speed Twister and Mother Reddy's location," Ashley suggested to Prince Jeff. Suddenly, a silhouette of Speed Twister appeared among the magic smoke. He was standing nearby an architecture that looked like an oval plan made of stone, tuff, and concrete behind him. "The description resembles the Colosseum; therefore, they are in Rome. Speed Twister looked lost in searching for the items," Prince Jeff said with his eyes closed.

Without wasting any time, Ashley took out her sword above her head …

Poof.

The three of them arrived in front of the historical Colosseum.

Bob was in awe looking at two muscular built men with an Ancient Rome war costume made from steel, holding a sword the same height as a man and holding a shield in red and silver colour.

Clink. Clink. The sound of sword clashes rang in their ears. Many spectators were cheering and clapping their hands for the fight.

"Where are we to start searching for Speed Twister and Mother Reddy or even the sacred ancient elements?" Ashley Sprinkler wondered while Prince Jeff and Bob stood with her.

"I need to touch Speed Twister's skin to activate my power of identification of the whereabouts of the sacred elements," Prince Jeff said.

"You can only identify the hidden ancient sacred elements precisely once you feel Speed Twister's skin?" Ashley asked.

"Yes, you understood correctly. The reason is that Speed Twister's emotion and latest information lies within his heart. By touching his skin, I can foresee the sacred items' whereabouts," Prince Jeff replied.

"Meanwhile, let me help you search for Speed Twister and Mother Reddy," Ashley responded.

Ashley closed her eyes, moving her sword in front of her and activating it. It shone brightly and showed Speed Twister and Mother Reddy's location; the background had many shoppers and tourists. When they saw a man in blue coloured skin and an enormous bird walk past, the shoppers' foreheads were visible with creased lines, and some of their hands were trembling.

Ashley's sword showed what caused tourists to be alarmed: Speed Twister and Mother Reddy walked towards a fountain. The ray of light from Ashley's sword showed the statue of Oceanus pulled by a chariot of two seahorses with water flowing in front of the statue.

"The architecture tells me that they are at Trevi Fountain. Let's go," Prince Jeff said.

In a flash, Ashley's sword brought them to Trevi Fountain.

Upon reaching their destination, Ashley, Prince Jeff, and Bob appeared standing at the doorstep of a souvenir shop that was opposite the fountain.

They heard someone saying, "Look! It's a man wearing a masquerade costume. This must be a new style for the year."

Speed Twister and Mother Reddy noticed people were calm and collected after hearing the statement that they were merely wearing the latest style clothing and mask.

"It is good that we are no longer the centre of their attention. Therefore, we can resume our search without being noticed. Let the search begin," Speed Twister said.

Both started to dive into the fountain in search of the sacred elements. Mother Reddy, having forgotten that she was in the form of a bird unable to breathe underneath the water, rose up and splashed water on shoppers and tourists as she flapped her enormous strong wings to dry.

Speed Twister got up from swimming and gave a signal to Mother Reddy to wait for him beside the Trevi Fountain overlooking the statue. Luckily for Speed Twister, he could live in any atmosphere; breathing in water was like breathing in air.

He shifted one stone to another, searching for the ancient sacred marbles. In his attempt to earnestly rummage for the marbles, he did not realize that his actions caused annoyance and upset the ancient statue spirit of the fountain. He disturbed the nicely placed façade by repositioning rocks while he underwent the search.

Within a few minutes or so while Speed Twister was concentrating on diving and searching from one end to another in the fountain in the crystal-clear water, the wild seahorse from the fountain statue shifted its head, and then its eyes opened widely.

Ashley, Prince Jeff, and Bob noticed it; all stood still seeing the change of events. “Did you both see that one of the statues is alive?” Ashley asked. Both replied that they did. “Let’s check out how an ancient statue could be alive. Its eyes opened widely as though it was furious.”

When they walked approaching the fountain, the other statue within its vicinity started to feel restlessness. Then, another statue, the God of Sea, started to move its head. Subsequently, like a rocket ship, the wild seahorse jumped into the water, splashing water out from the fountain, which hit Ashley’s dress, Prince Jeff’s top, and Bob’s fur. The three of them were flabbergasted.

The wild seahorse followed Speed Twister behind closely without Speed Twister even being aware of its presence. Every time Speed Twister turned his head as he felt something adhering to his movements, the seahorse pretended to be frozen and camouflaged itself amongst the other stones.

Nearly ten minutes in the water, when Speed Twister was about to return to the surface, the wild seahorse knocked Speed Twister's body with a significant impact that caused him to tumble down.

Then the God of the Sea statue got up and shifted its position from the arch of the Trevi Fountain. His Trident of Poseidon, which came out of from the side of his long cloth, was pointed at Speed Twister. The impact of the trident's power turned Speed Twister into a statue made of Carrara marble. He placed him at the centerpiece of the Trevi Fountain, replacing the statue of God of the Sea.

CHAPTER 14

The two seahorses (one was wild and another was docile) and the God of the Sea statue were alive, climbing down the Trevi Fountain façade and crossing the water. Their movements were fast; they swam across the fountain water within seconds and jumped out from the fountain and crashed into the chairs laid in front on the ground.

"Oh! No! Look at the statues. They are alive. Run for your life!" one of the shoppers screamed. The other tourists and shoppers scratched their heads, feeling disarray, some tears rolling down on their cheeks while some scrambled on the ground while trying to avoid or hide from the sudden mysterious occurrence.

Upon witnessing this, Ashley's hands turned to fists as she said to Prince Jeff, "I will protect the humans while you contain the impact from the mysterious statues."

Then she said, "Bracelet, release a large net." She pushed it towards a group of people lingering at the corner of the building on her left side, where the mystifying statue was about to ram them. Luckily, the magical net prevented the mystifying statue from passing and hurting the people.

They cheered at Ashley for her quick action and bravery.

Ashley smiled at them.

Prince Jeff and Bob ran as fast as their legs could take them by following the three mystifying statues with the plan to capture and turn them back to normal. Bob was courageous; he jumped on a table and landed on the docile seahorse body; his paw released his claws to clutch onto the statue. Unfortunately, since the statue was made from Carrara marble, Bob could not hold onto it without his paw being slippery.

Seeing what was happening to Bob, Prince Jeff released his magical digitalization power from his royal belt, pointing towards the seahorse's back, burning it and creating smoke. It neighed and momentarily stopped, looking in Prince Jeff's direction. Then it started to chase him.

Bob panted and quickly ran towards Prince Jeff's side to assist him.

The three mystifying statues abruptly stopped their movements to face Prince Jeff and Bob. The God of the Sea pointed its Trident of Poseidon towards both directions; its ray of light was about to hit both. Prince Jeff took out his royal sword and struck the ray of light which vanished in the thin air.

Bob placed his two paws against each other and said in his heart, "Ashley, please help us. We need you."

Ashley was helping calm the tourists and people around the Trevi Fountain when she heard the anguished murmur in her ears. "I must excuse myself. I need to help my friends."

She took her sword beside her, placed it above her head, and uttered a sentence, and *poof.* She appeared beside Prince Jeff in an instant.

She immediately shoveled her sword against the ray of lights. With the intense energy of the good-hearted sword magic, the magic sword managed to turn the ray of light into dust. Then, the mystifying statue huffed and puffed; it turned its head and walked away quickly.

"Where are they going?" Bob wondered. His body turned left and right.

"My hunch is that they are approaching the Spanish Steps; that is the nearest tourist attraction for them to make a row in public," Prince Jeff replied while shrugging.

"We must return them into their original forms to prevent more destruction or any fatality amongst civilians before we can save Speed Twister. By the way, what happened to Mother Reddy? I didn't notice her anywhere," Ashley said, feeling worried. She started biting her fingernails.

Prince Jeff and Bob nodded at the same time they shrugged while looking at Ashley.

All three of them ran, following the three mystifying statues. Ashley didn't command her sword to appear at the Spanish Steps since they had yet to determine the mystifying statues' plans and directions.

Those statues with their heaven materials crashed and knocked everything they passed by, ruining some traffic lights, and dented some transportation that hindered their movements. Finally, the wild seahorse took the lead for their journey and smashed some car windows as it passed by to signify his frustration.

Ashley, Prince Jeff, and Bob had to save some onlookers and humans trapped in their cars or busses.

Quickly thinking, Ashley uttered, "Bracelet, release net." The magic net appeared before her eyes, and she used her ring to place the safety net on high buildings to prevent the wild seahorse from smashing and collapsing them.

The three of them arrived at the Spanish Steps just as Prince Jeff guessed on the statues' next destination.

Many tourists and humans were lingering at the steep slope of steps and by Fontana Della Barcaccia. Ashley's fear materialized as the mystifying statues from the Trevi Fountain pushed tourists aside as they passed by. Since they were made of Carrara marble, their touch was uneven, leaving black bruises on onlookers and tourists.

Ashley and Prince Jeff could not utilize their powers in the crowded place, fearing that their powers may accidentally hit innocent civilians.

Bob jumped up and down excitedly when he saw something shining in the God of the Sea's mystifying statue eyes. He stood still and pointed his paw and his tail, starting to freeze in the statue's direction.

"Wait a minute, Bob, are you trying to inform us of something?" Ashley looked at his direction.

Bob repeated his movements happily and meowed. "I think there is an ancient sacred element hidden in the God of the Sea statue."

Prince Jeff took out his digital magnifying glasses, which showed him and Ashley the details of the statue's eyes. "There's a unique item in one of his eyes. It is shining. I guess we have to take that item first before we restore them," he said. "What are our plans to disperse all humans to safety? And to turn the statues back to normal?" Prince Jeff asked Ashley.

"I noticed that they are keen on reaching Fontana Della Barcaccia. Let's talk to the crowds using a portable voice amplifier. They should understand the urgency to vacate the Spanish Steps and Fontana Della Barcaccia in this situation. Let's give the mystifying statues an opportunity to reach the Fontana Della Barcaccia. Once they're there, we can use our powers to turn them into their original formation. What do you think?" Ashley suggested.

"Sounds like a splendid plan. Let's implement it now. No time to lose." Prince Jeff gave a thumbs up to Ashley.

"Bracelet, release portable voice amplifier." A portable voice amplifier promptly landed on Ashley's hand, and she smiled.

"Hi everyone, I am Ashley. I am making an emergency announcement. Your life is in danger since three bizarre and dangerous creatures are approaching. Please move away NOW!'"

Everyone in the crowd gathered their belongings and started to hurry away from the Spanish Steps. The majority ran or walked fast away from the Piazza di Spagna. Some remained stubborn and took out their cameras to snap photos of the three mystifying statues.

For those who didn't comply, Ashley had to use her magic and digital ring to place a digital rope around them to prevent them from moving forward closer to the mystifying statues. Then she used her sword's power to relocate them to a safer place at the end of the opposite road.

While Ashley guided the crowds to move away, Prince Jeff and Bob tried to distract the three mystifying statues from hurting or disturbing the public.

While waiting for the royal flying scooter to arrive, Prince Jeff commanded his magical and digitalization bracelet to distract the statue. On the other hand, Bob made a lot of fuss by meowing and scratching the mystifying statues' legs. They tried to stomp their heavy feet on Bob. Luckily for him, he was fast enough to jump away and run.

Unfortunately, the statue fell on the ground and make a shrieking sound.

Once Prince Jeff's royal flying scooter arrived, the mystifying statues forgot Bob's existence. They deviated their attention to the new object. The royal flying scooter flew fast, coming from the sky and then to the clouds, arriving to the Piazza di Spagna. Seeing his scooter approaching, Prince Jeff got ready his muscular and athletic legs, sprang into the air, and jumped on it.

The mystifying statues considered the flying scooter as a game. They tried to catch the scooter when it zoomed past. The God of the Sea extended his hands when the flying scooter passed before him and when the scooter flew to his back. He could not capture it since the royal flying scooter was driving too fast.

To ensure the crowds were safe, Ashley placed a strong magic net at each lane towards Piazza di Spagna. Once she was confident that the crowds were safe, she moved towards Prince Jeff and Bob's spot.

Ashley noticed Prince Jeff was distracting the mystifying statues in a game of catch me if you dare. "This game will be dangerous if the statue catches Prince Jeff, so I need to do something to distract them."

She whistled by using the amplifier to make her whistle sound louder for the mystifying statues to hear. All three of them stopped chasing Prince Jeff and turned their heads, appearing lost. Seeing this, she whistled for the second time to ensure they focused on her.

The whistle vibration shook the materials they were made from; it aggravated tremors within their heads, then their bodies until their legs. So they stopped momentarily, looked at each other, then scratched their heads.

Oh no! Did I aggravate their anger? Ashley thought to herself. She started breathing rapidly.

All three of their eyes turned red. Prince Jeff heard a loud, shrieking neigh coming from both seahorses.

"Run, Ashley! Run!" Prince Jeff and Bob shouted together.

CHAPTER 15

"I need to save Rome and put those mystifying statues back to where they belong, along with freeing Speed Twister and finding Mother Reddy. I have to be brave to face these adventures," Ashley said to herself.

With that in mind, she breath in deeply; next, she held her sword above her head and muttered a spell:

Only the generation of true heart grant me with great strength.

Sprinkle with love, sprinkle with heart.

Please give me the utmost magic to turn these mystifying statues into their original selves.

As she spoke, bright rays of purple and pink lights enveloped the sky just above her. Her brown hair curled, growing stripes of dark pink. Eventually, a pink filigree mask with rhinestones covered her face. In addition, her sword's pommel shone with white and blue light, which consisted of powerful good magic.

Seeing her transformation, Prince Jeff and Bob looked and smiled at each other and ran to her spot.

Ashley jumped high until she reached the same level as the three mystifying statues' heights. Then she shifted her hand, holding the magic sword from her side upwards and facing them. Consequently, the ray of white and blue light magic power emerged from the sword pommel and blinded the mystifying statues' eyesight.

"Ashley, do not do anything until we get hold of the God of the Sea's sacred eye," Prince Jeff told her telepathically when he placed two of his fingers at each side of his forehead.

Ashley nodded to his advice.

She stopped firing magic lights to fight against them. Instead, she appeared face to face with God of the Sea statue. "What do you want from me?" it asked Ashley.

"Kindly give me your sacred eye for us to break a curse." Ashley's opened her palm.

With its heavy hand made from Carrara marble, the God of the Sea statue punched at Ashley's face; the blow was strong and sent her backwards, leaving a red mark on her left cheek. She did somersaults through the air. As she tumbled down from the sky, she quickly said, "Bracelet, release net." A safety net appeared below her, and she fell gracefully without being hurt.

Seeing his friend get hurt, Prince Jeff, with his hand in a fist, quickly rode his royal flying scooter with Bob beside him. Once they reached the God of the Sea's eye level, he swayed his royal flying scooter from left to right of its head while honking noisily at it, disorienting the creature.

This caused the God of the Sea to raise his huge hands in an attempt to slap the royal scooter; however, it missed.

Then the scooter turned its direction to be closer to the God of the Sea's head. Bob, sitting quietly in the scooter, said, "I will try to claw its eyes to get hold of the sacred eye." Once he had an opening, Bob bravely jumped and landed on its forehead. Bob's buttocks were painful because the surface was made from hard materials. Nevertheless, he opened his claws to ensure his grip was secure.

"Will Bob be safe?" Prince Jeff wondered to himself.

Then he felt a rush of air passing by him. Turning his head, he saw Ashley holding her magic sword with her right hand and her auto-ring placed in her left hand shining and moving frantically to and fro within her middle finger. Then, instantaneously, the ring released a bright light that hit the God of the Sea statue's left arm.

The statue quickly moved its right arm to soothe its left arm by patting softly. Then, his heavy head turned to the left to look at the intensity of the injury.

While the attack caused him to deviate his attention, Bob took the opportunity to claw the sacred eye. Then Prince Jeff stopped his royal flying scooter at the same eye level as the God of the Sea; he took the opportunity to use his royal auto bracelet to release a laser to remove the sacred eye.

The God of the Sea subsequently moved his right arm towards his left eye once he felt a slight vibration. He intended to rub away the pain or obstacles that were bothering him, but before he could do so, Ashley called out, "Bracelet, release lasso stainless steel wire rope."

Poof.

It appeared in Ashley's hand. She hurriedly threw the lasso towards the God of the Sea statue's left hand, capturing it. Her eyes concentrated on moving his hand. Huffing and puffing, Ashley tightened her grip and pulled his hand aside. He then pushed his hands against the lasso's direction.

While Ashley tried her best to distract him, Prince Jeff and Bob managed to pull out the sacred eye and kept it in Prince Jeff's magic belt. Then both jumped onto the royal flying scooter.

Ashley, upon seeing her friends had completed their mission, said, "Bracelet, release the lasso."

Immediately, the God of Sea's hands touched the empty eye socket, and it started shrieking and wailing.

He turned his head and saw the royal flying scooter; without any hesitation, he jumped on the Spanish Steps with his heavy weight, breaking the stone and jumping up, trying to catch the scooter. He barely grazed it with his hand, making it wobble.

"Woah! Woah!" Bob cried out, almost falling off.

Ashley yelled, "Bracelet, release polyester lasso."

She threw it high up in the sky and, using her auto ring, made it circle Bob's waist and grip it firmly, and the magic lasso flew and placed Bob safely on the ground.

Prince Jeff's royal flying scooter shook severely. Then, smoke emerged and coughed. In order to save his life, Prince Jeff had no choice but to jump off from the flying scooter even though he was in the sky as high as forty-five feet.

Ashley yelled, "Bracelet, release parachute bag." Instantly, it appeared in Ashley's hand. She threw it in Prince Jeff's direction and cried out, "Parachute bag, please save Prince Jeff."

The parachute bag magically transported from Ashley's hand and appeared near Prince Jeff. Then it tried to roll into Prince Jeff's back to support him. After a few seconds, Prince Jeff managed to spring open two of his arms. The parachute bag wriggled onto Prince Jeff's arms and clasped at his chest. It opened its canopy just in time, leading Prince Jeff to land safely at the corner café. "Phew! That was a close call," Prince Jeff muttered under his breath while wiping away sweat.

The seahorses came rampaging towards Prince Jeff. As both of them were about to jump and hit him, Ashley managed to push Prince Jeff over to the other side of the café. While rolling on the pavement, she yelled, "Bracelet, release shelter!" Immediately, a transparent canopy covered them. The canopy consisted of electromagnetic waves that sent the mystifying statues bouncing away a few feet.

Ashley and Prince Jeff got up from their crouching positions upon seeing this. Both ran towards the Fontana Della Barcaccia. The God of the Sea lingered in the fountain, splashing water with his heavy hand. He seemed to be searching for something.

"My eyes! I cannot see without my eyes!" he shouted angrily.

"Is this what you are looking for?" Ashley asked him when Prince Jeff took out the sacred eye from his royal magic belt. It was shining due to the reflection of the sunshine; this blinded his vision as the ray of sun seeped into the only eye he had. Quickly, he covered his eye; he shifted his head to a place where there was no direct ray of sunlight.

Then he said, "Yes. That is my eye."

"God of the Sea, we took this to understand the uniqueness and usefulness of this sacred eye to break any curse. We would appreciate your explanation," Ashley said.

Before he managed to reply, the seahorse statues came over while stomping their heavy feet, which vibrated the items as they passed by.

Hearing the loud stomping noise and feeling the vibrations, Ashley and Prince Jeff looked in the direction where both the seahorses were coming from.

Within a few feet nearing the Fontana Della Barcaccia, the two seahorses jumped from their spot, galloping in the sky with their strong feet. Within a flash, they landed, splashing the Fontana Della Barcaccia's water.

Ashley and Prince Jeff were lucky to jump away from the fountain and remain at a safe distance.

The ray of sunlight blinded the three mystifying statues, emanating light from the sacred eyeball Ashley was holding.

Once the ray of sunlight and the magic in the sacred eye shone on them, they vanished into thin air.

"What … what happened? Where are they?" Ashley exclaimed, turning her head and body to search for them. Ashley flew by using her magic sword from one corner lane to another of Piazza di Spagna.

"This is weird. They are no longer within this vicinity," she said.

Prince Jeff and Bob ran towards the Fontana Della Barcaccia, checking on the ground nearby their shoes just in case the statues became smaller. However, there was no trace of them.

Both looked puzzled and were breathing heavily since both were amazed and concerned about the whereabouts of the mystifying statues.

Prince Jeff, located at the foot of the Spanish Steps, felt an intense pain on his forehead. "Ouch," he said. Then he bent forward and crouched on the ground.

Bob noticed this and quickly ran to his side. He asked, "Why are you suddenly in pain?"

Prince Jeff extended his right arm to touch the tip of his broad forehead. Out of the blue, a blurry vision emerged from his royal magic belt. It flickered, along with an electronic buzzing sound, and then it died.

Bob placed his paw on the royal magic belt to find the mysterious source. Then he remembered the sacred eye. It must have been the item that bothered Prince Jeff. Maybe it wanted to share a clue of the whereabouts of the statue since Prince Jeff was the only creature that could foresee or view the whereabouts of any mystifying or magic items.

Bob relayed to Prince Jeff the hunch he made with that analysis of what was happening. Trusting Bob's hunch, Prince Jeff opened his royal magic belt to take out the sacred eye. As he held it, the eye emanated a ray of shining bright lights, blinding Prince Jeff and Bob momentarily. Again, the blurry vision emerged through Prince Jeff's forehead; later, it was clear.

Prince Jeff closed his eyes to deviate from the intense shining ray of lights. Then the vision became more apparent and robust. He raised his royal sword above his head, which released the specific location of the three mystifying statues. His vision also indicated that the sacred eye was not the item that Speed Twister was searching to break the Three Weird Sisters' curse.

"Argh," Prince Jeff uttered once the vision vanished, and he panted due to the intense energy utilized to look at the items. "The mystifying statues are at the Colosseum."

Bob jumped up and down. He started to feel anxious and whispered, "Ashley! Ashley, where are you? We need to be at the Colosseum." He repeated this three times under his breath, and then he walked to and fro since he was desperately seeking her help. "Help us, Ashley, please!"

Ashley could hear his desperate cry for help and flew over to them.

Then she turned to look at Prince Jeff, who was slouching with his eyes closed as he rubbed his temples.

She told him, "What you said earlier is accurate; it does take a lot of your energy to foresee the ancient sacred items."

She placed her true heart sword above Prince Jeff's head and uttered a spell:

Only the generation of true heart,

Grant me with great strength.

A strong grip shifted her sword aside, and a soft palm covered her mouth. Prince Jeff scolded her, "Stop, Ashley, I don't require your magic to regain my strength. Thanks for your thoughts."

Then with his two hands clapping together, a ball of lights emerged from his hands and moved fast like a bullet train to cover his body. With that procedure, Prince Jeff was finally standing sturdy, and his eyes were attentive.

"Let's go and save Speed Twister and Mother Reddy before we turn the mystifying statues into their original selves," Ashley suggested.

Suddenly, they saw a huge bird flying in the sky. "It's Mother Reddy!" Bob exclaimed excitedly.

Prince Jeff talked to Mother Reddy telepathically, "The mystifying statues are at the Colosseum. If you are here to assist us in undoing the spell and free Speed Twister, please join us."

Mother Reddy flew at a low height the same level as them, passed by, and flew away.

CHAPTER 16

Mother Reddy ignored Prince Jeff's suggestion while she flew past the Fontana Della Barcaccia, where Ashley, Prince Jeff, and Bob were standing. To everyone's surprise, her beak snatched the sacred eye from Prince Jeff's palm, and then she sped away.

"Let's go, Ashley; we need to save Rome from mass destruction." Prince Jeff pulled Ashley's hand.

She nodded. Bob jumped in agreement.

When Ashley was about to raise her magic sword above her head, Mother Reddy's shadow flew by once more.

"Witchery Minister, please send me another royal flying scooter, as the previous scooter was destroyed," Prince Jeff called via his auto-bracelet.

While three of them were getting ready for their next journey and place, Mother Reddy arrived at Trevi Fountain; she let go of her claws that were holding the sacred eye of the God of the Sea. It hit the Speed Twister statue's head, which was made of Carrara marble. The marble was gradually broken into pieces, falling into the fountain water bit by bit. This revealed Speed Twister, whereby he wriggled both of his arms and jumped beside the Trevi fountain statue.

"It's great to be free. Good job, Mother Reddy." He clapped his hand. "Let's not waste our time. We need to find the three sacred marbles. According to my instincts, they may be hidden at the grounds of the Colosseum amphitheatre."

***

Meanwhile, at the Colosseum, Ashley uttered the magic words. "Sword, transport us to Trevi Fountain."

"Woah! Why Trevi?" Prince Jeff asked before all three of them vanished and appeared at Trevi Fountain. Its surroundings were upside down due to the God of the Sea and Speed Twister breaking the marbles when freed.

Once they arrived, Prince Jeff looked at Ashley with his jaw tightened upon seeing the condition of Trevi Fountain was a mess.

"My hunch is accurate; Mother Reddy did it again. She has undone the spell placed on Speed Twister. Look, there is a hole on the centerpiece of the Trevi Fountain." Ashley pointed at the hole.

The tourists and shoppers saw Ashley, and then they pulled her sleeves and said, "Girl, a huge bird flew and stopped momentarily at the side of the fountain. Next, she threw an eye-looking stone on a statue. The weird part is that we saw the statue materials broke into pieces, revealing a blue skinned man with his hair in a shape of meatballs. He woke up and ran away." One of them was biting their fingers and their hands were trembling while talking.

"Did you see or hear where they are planning to go from here?" Ashley inquired.

"The Colosseum. The blue-faced man mentioned it," one of the shoppers said and nodded.

"Thank you for the information. Please call the 'la polizia' to settle the messy and unrest condition," Ashley advised.

***

In Desperate Valley, Angie, the only witch with engineering capabilities amongst the Three Weird Sisters, tried to fix their magic crystal ball since it was broken into pieces by her quick-tempered sister Danielle.

"How are we to track and help Speed Twister find the ancient sacred items fast without us detecting the items' whereabouts?"

"We are trapped in our realms for years and years. Look at my hair! There is white visible; my power and youthfulness are reducing since I have not being using my evil power outside our realm!" Danielle screamed and threw harshly an embroidered cushion on the floor.

"Stop complaining. Danielle and Cindy, come ignite each of our powers to repair the broken magic crystal ball."

All three of them stood in a circle, holding each other's hands, and then they moved clockwise three times; Angie muttered some spells as they moved.

"Close your eyes, then count to ten. Please raise your hands together," Angie said to her sisters.

After doing so, all three of them raised their hands simultaneously. The broken glass pieces were dancing in the air, swapping places until they were placed in the proper section, like completing a puzzle board game.

Then all three of them opened their eyes and brought their hands down, ensuring not to break the fixing spell. Then, Angie said another spell, whereby magic dust covered the crystal ball, circling a few times. Finally, the magic crystal ball looked brand-new.

"Yes, we did it!" Angie exclaimed excitedly.

Without any delay, Danielle suggested igniting the two ancient elements from Shanghai and Kuala Lumpur. "Let's negotiate for their assistance."

Cindy and Angie nodded in agreement.

Danielle pointed both of her fingers towards the ancient Chinese wristwatch and the tips of Towers One and Two of KLCC.

"One, two, three!" They all raised their palms facing upwards. Upon reaching mid-air above their chests, they began to flip their palms, their skinny index fingers pointing at the two items placed beside the bowl.

Danielle, Angie, and Cindy uttered a spell. "Arbralililoath Bibibowbow."

They placed the two ancient sacred items side by side in the bowl. A sudden gust of wind passed by their faces, and then a twirl of wind, along with small lightning.

The fierce dragon silhouette appeared large within a few seconds, and the distorted lady in white with long black hair emerged from the bowl.

"Why do you summon us this time?" both said together.

"We need your help to find the last ancient sacred elements in Europe. Which part of Rome?" Danielle pleaded.

"I am sorry. We can only identify and feel the very presence of the last sacred items once we combine them with the third sacred item. At the moment, both of us are powerless."

Hearing this, both returned to their sacred items, leaving Danielle, Cindy, and Angie thinking the next course of action.

"Let's put the message across to Speed Twister. He has to return with the ancient sacred items found in Sydney for the dragon and the 'Pontianak' to be able to determine the last ancient sacred item's whereabouts," Danielle said.

She raised her arms with her palms facing upwards, facing the beaded ceiling decorated with a toffee crystal chandelier. Her hands moved in a circle, making a transparent ball.

She said, "DahhlieexistDahlieexistica."

Speed Twister was holding his magic pen, trying to identify any ancient sacred items hidden in the grounds of Colosseum. While concentrating, he felt his hair and the sand be blown aside.

"Mother Reddy, look, there is a message."

The message said:

"Speed Twister, please return with the ancient sacred items from Sydney. The magical spirit from the two sacred items, Mr. Dragon and Ms. Pontianak, require the third ancient sacred element from Sydney to be near them for them to identify the exact location of the last ancient sacred element."

After reading aloud, the wind blew the wordings, replacing them with sand.

He closed his opened mouth with his hands.

"Unbelievable, Mother Reddy, we have the leads in our hands."

He started clapping his hands.

"Mother Reddy, we need to return to Desperate Valley and share the ancient koala and kangaroo sacred teeth and nails that we found hidden in Australia for the two magical spirits to identify the exact location of the last ancient sacred element."

She looked at Speed Twister, then flipped her enormous, strong wings up and down.

"Wait! Please let me sit on your wing first before you flap your wings faster." Speed Twister ran as he hurried to jump onto Mother Reddy's flapping wings. He nearly missed the flat spot as he was about to sit. He was lucky his skinny old hand managed to grab some of Mother Reddy's feathers.

A wind blew some sand, and suddenly Ashley, Prince Jeff, and Bob appeared at the ground that Speed Twister and Mother Reddy were standing.

"Where do you think you're going?" Ashley asked with her sword pointed in Speed Twister's direction.

"Home, of course, dearie." He smiled while holding the tip of his moustache. Then off they went.

Her sword released a ray of bright light that burned the tip of Mother Reddy's buttocks feathers; smoke emerged, which reduced her speed.

Speed Twister's face turned to slight red upon seeing Ashley trying her best to stop them from flying.

Then he stood tall on Mother Reddy's wing. He took out two of his magical pens and uttered a magic spell. Then, he twisted and turned his magical pens, repairing her feathers.

"Ashley is starting to be naughty, bullying an old man."

He uttered a magic spell, and his right hand holding a magic pen released an electric red ray of light that blinded Ashley, Prince Jeff, and Bob. Unfortunately, it was too sudden that Ashley didn't command any of her digital and magical artifacts for their assistance.

Due to that, the electric red ray of light consisting of evil magic cuffed and gripped Ashley and Prince Jeff. Consequently, it froze all their digital and magical artifacts. Ashley coughed and opened her mouth for air to come into her lungs.

Ashley told Prince Jeff, "At the count of five, let's push and kick the magical grip simultaneously so we can use our power."

After counting, Ashley and Prince Jeff used all their strength to push the evil magic that gripped away from their bodies while activating their digital and magical artifacts. Both with the ray of good-hearted white light emanating from their artifacts fought with the evil red lights; however, it died on their first attempt. The evil red magic was powerful and caused Ashley to lose her strength and energy.

"Ashley, wake up. Are you alright? Please speak to me." Prince Jeff's heartbeat moved fast; he inhaled deeply to remain calm, seeing Ashley was lightheaded and feeling queasy then. She closed her eyes; however, her chest was still moving up and down. "Phew! Luckily, she is still breathing. I guess she is closing her eyes due to a loss of energy."

Bob was lucky to be at a shorter height than both of them, therefore he was able to avoid the magic spell. When he saw the ray of light was about to hit Ashley and Prince Jeff, he managed to hide behind a huge sandy rock beside her.

CHAPTER 17

"Ha ha ha!" Speed Twister laughed at Ashley and Prince Jeff; his wicked magic had paralyzed both of them.

Mother Reddy's wings flapped hurriedly at high speed. Then off they flew past the Colosseum, then beyond the messy Trevi Fountain. Next, they flew higher into the sky crowded with puffy clouds.

"Move aside, you irritating clouds. You are making my journey a bumpy one," Speed Twister said, annoyed.

"Woah!"

Mother Reddy bumped into huge, thick clouds as she was about to leave planet Earth. Adamantly wishing to be freed from this planet, she pushed herself against the clouds and strong winds. She kept on flapping her wings vigorously. Although Speed Twister was not stable in this situation since he was sitting on her left wing, seeing lots of thick clouds and the bumpy ride, he managed to move to the center of Mother Reddy's body.

"That is better," he said to himself.

***

At the Colosseum, after witnessing Ashley and Prince Jeff were under Speed Twister's wicked spell, Bob closed his eyes and placed his paws together and prayed. "Witchery Minister and Billy, please come and save us. Please, we need your help." His tail was on sweeping the ground.

After countless minutes of praying and wailing, Bob heard, "*Zoom, zoom, zoom!*"

Bob opened his eyes, seeing an object flying fast from one cloud to another. Then, inch by inch, the object grew more prominent; it had the silhouette of a scooter.

"Look, there is a flying scooter heading this way. Stand back and hide at a safer place!" One person pointed and hurried to hide behind a worn-out sandy stone.

Hearing this, Ashley shook her head. She managed to regain her energy after closing her eyes to recharge. Prince Jeff opened his eyes widely, looking at the sky. Ashley tried to move her hands again, hoping to break free, but she could not move a muscle. Finally, she tried to utter, "Bracelet, release shelter." But nothing happened. Her bracelet was not shining since it was under Speed Twister's wicked spell of paralyzing.

Prince Jeff shared the same fate as Ashley this time.

Bob sat aside and continued closing his eyes with tears rolling onto his furry cheeks. "Please, Witchery Minister. Please, Billy. We need your help urgently."

A few feet away in the sky, Bob opened one of his eyes to see whether the object was about to hit and damage the entire Colosseum. To his pleasant surprise, he saw a long, creamy-coloured robe with the Goodness Realm's royal emblem embedded on the front of the scooter.

"Witchery Minister! You are here to save us. Hooray!" Bob was jumping up and down with his whiskers pushed forward.

A few feet before landing at the grounds of Colosseum, Bob noticed that Witchery Minister was holding a long walking stick with the Goodness Realm's royal emblem on it.

He knocked the stick three times on the royal flying scooter. Then he pointed the long stick in Prince Jeff and

Ashley's direction. A speck of magic dust appeared, lingering above Prince Jeff and Ashley's heads, then to their necks, circling to their bodies, and ending at their feet. The magic dust pushed aside the evil magic cuff surrounding both of them.

In return, not accepting defeat, the evil magic cuff retaliated by pushing against the magic dust far away. The evil magic cuff was about to circle and surround Ashley and Prince Jeff again when all clear from the magic gripped. Ashley, quick in her response, placed her sword facing the evil magic cuff, and she uttered a few spells. Thus, the evil magic cuff vanished into the air.

After that, Witchery Minister knocked the walking stick three times, and Ashley's good-hearted sword power, then Prince Jeff's royal sword, united as one powerful magic. The magic engulfed the sky, causing the wind and clouds to twirl and turn to an indigo colour.

It was so powerful that the twirling wind pulled Mother Reddy fiercely into the wind. Speed Twister managed to jump off of Mother Reddy, tumbling and rolling in the sky.

He quickly took out two of his magic pens and said some spells; this led him to disappear and appear at the leaning tower where the mystifying status of Trevi Fountain gathered.

"No, no, no! I need to return to Desperate Valley, not here!" Speed Twister shouted, stomping his foot on the ground.

***

"Unbelievable, Mother Reddy and Speed Twister didn't drop down from the sky straight to our location when we retaliated against his evil power!" Ashley said, looking dismayed.

Once their magic power dispersed from the sky, they could see the silhouette of Mother Reddy.

She was flapping her wings up and down. She did not fall down due to the assistance of her magic that she uttered when she was within the twirl. Now, she flew as fast as she could, trying to determine the whereabouts of Speed Twister.

"Mother Reddy! Come this instant. I am at the leaning tower!" Speed Twister cried out, using his two magic pens to transport his message by using the waves of sound; within a few seconds, the message arrived in Mother Reddy's ear.

Oh my! It is 266 km away up north away from Rome. That will be quite a journey against the strong wind, Mother Reddy thought. Her heartbeat started to beat rapidly on this thought.

She flapped her wings up and down along with her buttocks feathers to quicken her movements and speed to fly in a haste.

"Did you see that? Mother Reddy is flying faster than her usual speed. I have the deepest feeling that Speed Twister is asking her to save him," Prince Jeff said while observing Mother Reddy's silhouette moving in the sky.

CHAPTER 18

"Without the sacred eye from the God of the Sea, the mystifying statue, I cannot foresee the location of the statue, Speed Twister, and the last sacred items whereabouts accurately," Prince Jeff said. "The last I saw, the sacred items that Speed Twister is searching for are at the Leaning Tower of Pisa," he added, sighing.

"What are we waiting for? Let's go to Pisa." Ashley got up hurriedly.

***

At the large garden beside leaning tower of Pisa, crowds dispersed, running out of control, trying to find a safe place to hide when they saw the three mystifying statues alive, stomping their feet while walking, which caused the ground to quake.

They were abruptly interrupted by Speed Twister's sudden appearance, which annoyed them.

"Go away, you mad man!" said the God of the Sea with his hand shooing him.

Speed Twister scurried away when he saw the God of the Sea was about to take out his trident of Poseidon, which came from the side of his long cloth. The trident was facing him.

He muttered a spell and found himself in the administration ticketing building.

Well, I should be safe here while waiting for Mother Reddy to arrive, Speed Twister thought to himself.

Then he felt the teeth and nails of the sacred items from Sydney were chiming and crunching, making many noises in his pocket.

He put his hands into his pants pocket to take out the items. To his surprise, he felt a burning sensation when he touched them.

"What on Earth?" he whispered to himself.

He took out one of his magic pens and pointed it in the direction of his pants' pocket to stop the items from shuddering, chiming, and crunching.

Instead, his magic pen power managed to take it out gracefully from his pocket. Once the items were out and controlled by his magic pen, his mouth fell open, and then he blinked his eyes and rubbed them.

"Am I dreaming?" He pinched the top of his hands.

At the administrative building where he was sitting on a bench, he looked up and saw a window. He placed his right hand over his chin; then he got up and stood on his legs to look over the windowsill.

He stared open mouthed. The three mystifying statues turned to their original selves. They turned into concrete. Did it correlate with the ancient sacred items from Sydney? He massaged his moustache while thinking.

"Let me experiment with it."

He twisted and turned his hands while holding two of his magic pens. Finally, he uttered a spell to stop his magic pen surrounding and controlling the sacred items.

The three mystifying statues opened their eyes and started making lots of noises like huffing and puffing. Then, they began throwing benches and running here and there in the garden grounds like mad dogs.

"Next, if my magic pen is to control the sacred items, does this make them obedient or do they become motionless like their original statue versions?" he thought aloud.

He commanded his magic pen to control the sacred items from Sydney; as per his hunch, the three mystifying statues stood still within a few seconds, and then they returned to their original selves. The God of the Sea, flanked by the two seahorses, did not move a muscle at the foot of the leaning tower, the same decoration and position that they held at Trevi Fountain.

This is fun; I can control them, he thought to himself while smiling and twirling his moustache.

Then, above the rooftop of the administration building, the sound of a caw rang in Speed Twister's ears.

"Is it Mother Reddy? Is she here already?" he thought aloud.

Speed Twister scurried to the entrance, extending his height, trying to look at who made the sound.

Then, a shadow of an enormous bird flew past beside the building.

"What took you so long?" He smiled.

"Caw, caw," Mother Reddy replied.

Her wings flapped up and down excitedly.

"Run along. We are behind time. I found an interesting fact about the ancient sacred items from Sydney. We can control those three mystifying statues with these sacred items." Speed Twister spoke to Mother Reddy while he jumped onto her wings and then rolled himself onto her back.

Her enormous strong wings started to flap up and down to gear up for a flight away from Earth.

Suddenly, Ashley and Prince Jeff emerged at the entrance of the administration building face to face with Speed Twister holding their magic swords.

"Hold on, Speed Twister," Ashley pleaded with her sword pointing at his direction.

"What is there to discuss, dearie? For sure, you are unable to break the curse with your magic sword nor your digital artifacts to help my nieces trapped in their realms." He turned, facing Ashley with a fist on his hands.

"Where are the three mystifying statues?" Prince Jeff asked Speed Twister.

"Ha!" He twisted and turned his two magic pens; after that, the sound of roaring and commotion came from the direction of the Leaning Tower of Pisa.

"Can you hear their voices? They are outside within Pisa area."

"Happy fighting." Speed Twister chuckled at Ashley and Prince Jeff. Mother Reddy flew high up in the sky and then both of them vanished.

Ashley was about to point her sword towards their direction and utter a spell; however, a strong resistance by a long stick prevented her.

"Let them go, Ashley. He needs to save his niece from their evil and greedy needs. We are here to protect the planet Earth and other realms," Witchery Minister advised Ashley and Prince Jeff.

CHAPTER 19

Witchery Minister pointed his magic walking stick above the sky, pointing in Mother Reddy's direction. It glowed and showed the location of the sacred eye. It dropped beneath the Trevi Fountain after releasing Speed Twister from his statue state.

"Guess we have to retrieve the item for Prince Jeff to determine the location of the last sacred items and Speed Twister's next journey." Witchery Minister winked.

Next, at the foot of the administration building of the Leaning Tower of Pisa, Ashley exclaimed, "Did you see that? Speed Twister woke up the lifeless three mystifying statues, which means he can control them with the koala and kangaroo ancient sacred items that he got in Sydney."

The three of them stood and looked at the statue.

"You are observant, Ashley," Prince Jeff replied. Then he started to massage his forehead, thinking.

"Since Speed Twister is gone, we cannot revert them to normal?" Bob asked.

"Shall I go to Desperate Valley to borrow the items from him?" Ashley asked at this suggestion.

Prince Jeff rolled his eyes in response to this.

"That is a bad suggestion, Ashley," Witchery Minister added with his index finger was moving left and right.

"Why not we try both magical swords, along with the magic walking stick, to lure them to return to Trevi Fountain?" Ashley's eyes twinkled.

"That is a better option. Let's do it." Prince Jeff smiled.

"The three mystifying statues are currently amok with three of them punching each other and smashing the wall on top of the Leaning Tower," Prince Jeff said while he strained his eyes, trying to see the three figures from where he was standing.

***

Returning to Desperate Valley realm from planet Earth was a perilous journey.

Once they flew high up in the sky, passing several clouds along with thunder and lightning that nearly burnt Mother Reddy's feathers, Speed Twister was supposed to use his magic pen to appear in Desperate Valley. However, both were thrown to the last layer of Earth (the exosphere) due to bad weather.

"Oh my! Mother Reddy, we are close to space. Look at the moon over there," Speed Twister said in a nervous voice. "Let me think of a spell for us to return to Desperate Valley."

He twisted and turned his wrists, holding the two magical pens, and uttered a magical spell. The first attempt was a failure. His fingers were trembling, and he was sweating.

He sighed. "Mother Reddy, I am at a loss of the correct spells to leave this atmosphere."

He shook his head and rubbed his forehead.

They could not return to Earth nor proceed towards space; therefore, both lingered in the small area between Earth and space.

"Mother Reddy, it looks like we are temporarily stuck here until my dear nieces detect us." He slouched, and his moustache faced downwards.

***

"Magic crystal ball, show yourself," Danielle commanded with her fingers calling them. "What is taking Speed Twister and Mother Reddy so long to arrive at Desperate Valley?"

The crystal ball showed that both were stuck in between the layers of Earth and space.

"They are lost!" Danielle opened her mouth widely while her sisters scratched their hair.

"Strange, Speed Twister can go in and out anywhere on Earth, along with other realms without any difficulties," Danielle responded while fidgeting her nails.

"How can we help them in this situation?" Angie pondered while walking to and fro.

"Let's seek assistance from the Maiden of Maze Realm." Cindy got up from her seat abruptly.

"Good idea, Cindy," Danielle and Angie responded.

"Magic crystal ball, magic crystal ball, come to me."

Cindy raised her arms with her palms facing the beaded ceiling decorated with a toffee crystal chandelier. Her hands moved in a small circle that created a transparent ball.

She said, "DahhlieexistDahlieexistica."

In the Maze Realm, Lady Maiden of the Maze Realm was busy developing and prototyping new toys and games for the next Christmas. She was in her production room located at the realm's edge. Her most trusted subjects, Barbie Day & Night and Sergeant from the army toys realms, were with her.

She was using her sceptre along with her magic fingers; a baby doll appeared on the pavement above the marble floor.

Then Barbie Day & Night walked towards the pavement to pick it up for Lady Maiden of the Maze Realm to implement a thorough inspection on her antique wooden table. As Barbie approached the table and placed the prototype doll on it, all of a sudden, the Three Weird Sisters' silhouettes appeared at the centre of the table. The sudden appearance startled both Lady Maiden of the Maze Realm and Barbie Day & Night, and thus they dropped their prototype. In a flash, Lady Maiden held her sceptre tightly, subsequently pointing at the silhouettes, getting ready to attack if required to do so. Then the silhouettes formed into the Three Weird Sisters.

"Hi Lady of Maiden, how are you? Remember us? Danielle, Cindy, and Angie," the Three Weird Sisters greeted in their sweetest voices.

"No one can forget the three beautiful sisters." Lady of Maiden mouth curved upwards. "My, oh my, you found another way to communicate with me. Very charming that the three of you are innovative. Maybe one day you can join my toys development team." Her index finger was pointing at their direction.

"Run along and spill the beans. I have tons of projects to settle." Lady of Maiden opened two of her arms to allow them to speak.

"We seek your assistance to bring Speed Twister back. The enormous bird, Mother Reddy, and he are stuck in the exosphere." Angie's hands clasped together, and Cindy's upper lip curled into a scowl.

"The exosphere? You meant he was on planet Earth? The most difficult planet to live in as well as to fly to and fro?" She glanced up the ceiling while her nose crinkled.

After that, she walked back and forth with her head tilted, looking downwards. Her left hand was folded at her back, another hand holding the sceptre. Then she stopped and turned her head up. Her dark black eyes with a touch of orange colour concentrated on the Three Weird Sisters.

"The only living being other than humans that can survive on planet Earth's atmosphere is life being from the Maze Realm since we produce toys and games for their festive seasons, having businesses contracts with those greedy humans." She balled her fist.

"Argh!" Both of her hands were squeezing both sides of her head, tousling her beautifully braided hair as she shook her head.

"I have no choice but to save the old man and the bird myself! This is a waste of my time!" Lady of Maiden shouted.

The Three Weird Sisters smiled. "What are your plans, Lady Maiden of the Maze Realm?"

"You can see it with your eyes if you remain attentive of your magic crystal ball." The corner of her eyes crinkled while she waived her sceptre.

She raised her right hand while holding the sceptre, then twisted the sceptre's head with her wrist in a clockwise motion.

She muttered a spell, and then her black eye with a tint of orange colour turned to full dark orange. It encompassed her pupils, and they turned to silver. Bright orange ray of lights emerged from her eyes, and then all her body raised high up near the magic office's ceiling.

Within a few seconds, an intense whirlwind in greyish colour formed at the top ceiling of the magic office. It looked as though the whole place was about to be sucked by the intense wind.

Barbie Day & Night and the Sergeant grabbed hold of the bulky antique table to prevent them from being absorbed by the tornado.

Lady Maiden of the Maze Realm vanished in the blink of an eye within the whirlwind located on the ceiling. The room was left quiet like a dead tomb.

The Three Weird Sisters clapped their hands. "Speed Twister to the rescue," Danielle whispered to herself.

She twisted her wrists, and then they no longer had the accessibility to view the Maze Realm.

"We will reconnect later to get the updates," Danielle told her sisters.

***

"Well, well, well, look who is relaxing without having any guts to plan for return." So, Lady Maiden, with her forehead puckered, talked face to face at Speed Twister while he was dozing off, hidden between Mother Reddy's thick feathers.

He nearly fell off from his cosy sleeping place when he saw Lady Maiden's face close to him, and he could smell her orange-scented breath. "I must be dreaming." He rubbed his eyes and blinked twice. "Are you real, Lady Maiden?"

He scrambled and jolted up from his sleeping position.

"I am here to rescue you, as per your nieces' request. Come, let's go. We have no time to waste!" Lady Maiden shouted with her hands shaking here and three.

"Mother Reddy, I told you so, my nieces are responsible in seeking assistance," Speed Twister replied.

"Both hold still together as the wind of my sceptre is strong against planet Earth's atmosphere. So, you may fall back and miss the chance to be transported to Desperate Valley and remain on Earth," Mother Reddy instructed.

Hearing this, Speed Twister grabbed hold of Mother Reddy's feathers; then she raised her right hand while holding the sceptre, twisting the sceptre's head with her wrist in a clockwise motion. Her mouth was muttering a spell, and then her black eye with a tint of orange colour turned to full dark orange. It encompassed her pupils, which then turned to silver. Bright orange ray of lights emerged from her eyes, and then her body raised high up. All three of them vanished in the blink of an eye within the whirlwind.

The three appeared in front of the Three Weird Sisters within a split second. Their entrance was sudden and surprising, and the current from the magical tornado was strong and caused The Three Weird Sisters' hair to flip, and their clothes were blown backward.

The Three Weird Sisters were ready with their magical fingers pointing towards the tornado, about to cast a spell if an intruder were to appear. However, their magical ray of light sparks from their magical fingers stopped instantly when they saw Speed Twister, Lady Maiden, and Mother Reddy.

"It's just us, Danielle, Cindy, and Angie. Thanks to Lady Maiden and yourself, Mother Reddy and I are safe," Speed Twister said while holding the tip of his moustache with his white teeth sparkling.

"That was close!" Danielle relaxed her shoulders.

"Welcome back! Thank you, Lady Maiden of Maze Realm, for rescuing both of them," Danielle said.

"I will go off now since I have lots of Maze Realms matters to settle," Lady Maiden said while smiling at them.

Danielle, known for her impatience, snatched Sydney's ancient sacred items using her skinny magical right-hand finger to take them out from Speed Twister's pocket. Due to her haste of snatching the items, one of the four items accidentally dropped on the marble floor. Luckily, it rolled and rolled until Angie used her magic finger to halt the item, the kangaroo teeth, from rolling.

Danielle smacked her palm against her forehead.

"I told you several times, Danielle, you need to have more patience with these ancient items. They are fragile, and we need to handle them with care." Speed Twister glared at Danielle while scolding.

Angie skilfully placed the kangaroo teeth into the magic crystal bowl. Then Danielle placed all the remaining items into the magic crystal bowl side by side with the items from Shanghai and Kuala Lumpur.

Then Danielle pointed both of her fingers towards the ancient Chinese wristwatch and the tips of Towers One and Two of KLCC.

"Wait! We should not mix all of them in the crystal bowl!" Speed Twister shouted with his right palm facing outwards.

"Why?" Two of Danielle's shoulders raised.

"Wouldn't it annoy the spirits in the ancient sacred items?" Speed Twister responded.

Cindy replied, "Remember that they informed us that they can identify and feel the exact presence of the last sacred items once the spirits are able to feel the presence of the third sacred items."

Danielle and Angie nodded in agreement.

"Then run along and combine all the items," Speed Twister replied.

"One, two, three." They raised their palms facing upwards. Upon reaching mid-air above their chests, they began to flip their palms, their skinny index fingers pointing at the six items placed inside the bowl. Then, Danielle, Angie, and Cindy uttered a spell, "Arbralililoath Bibibowbow."

The fierce dragon silhouette appeared large, along with a distorted lady in a white dress with long black hair with sharp fangs.

"We can feel the presence of the third ancient sacred item," both chorused.

A fierce Bunyip in a muddy green colour—tail like a crocodile and body like a snake or furry human with its long tongue stuck out—appeared beside those two magical elements. *"Roar. Roar!"*

"Why and who woke me up?" His eyebrow tilted aside.

"It's us, the Three Weird Sisters and Speed Twister, witches from Desperate Valley and the Maze Realm. We woke you up to assist us in searching for the ancient sacred element hidden in Eastern Europe believed to be in Rome," Angie replied while curtsying.

The dragon and the Pontianak faced the Bunyip; the Bunyip looked at them with its long tongue sticking out, its saliva dripping. Then it said, "The only way for us to foresee the fourth ancient sacred element is to join our hands and mind together." Subsequently, he raised his arms.

The Pontianak said, "Let's join hands in a circle next to the table located by the crystal bowl." Both nodded in agreement. Once all three of them were ready to touch each other, they walked in a circle like a merry-go-round, saying their spells. After ten rounds of circling, crystal bowl at the centre, a wisp of smoke shrouded it. Then an ancient marble silhouette appeared before their eyes, one black intertwined with silver lying on a bed of water somewhere at Trevi Fountain. Another piece that looked sapphire blue intertwined with black was hidden at the "Tugu Negara" in Kuala Lumpur.

Poof.

The wisp of smoke died like a human's breath blew it.

"What about the last marble? Where is it located?" Danielle shouted, rolling her eyes.

Hearing this, the dragon released fire from his mouth as his face turned red like a cherry. "I've had enough of your impatient attitude!" Then a few fireballs came out from his mouth, one after another in Danielle's direction.

Danielle, Cindy, and Angie were on guard; they were ready with their magical powers; they retaliated by squeezing all their fingers. This action caused their magic to choke and shake the dragon. The dragon suffocated; his tail was wriggling and kicking here and there.

"I will continue this mission," he managed to say while he tried to fight against the evil magic gripping his throat.

Seeing the dragon give up in retaliation, Three Weird Sisters stopped their spells. Then the dragon could breathe normally again.

The three ancient magical spirits re-started their rituals after touching each other and walking in a circle; accordingly, the crystal bowl engulfed in a smoke. The last marble had a blood-red background with a knife picture on its centrepiece. The scenery was blinking; then it went blank, and finally more smoke flared up from the bowl. Next, they could see butterfly flower bushes with Delphinium flowers in a garden, then a blue swing standing majestically on a bed of nicely trimmed green grass.

"Where is this?" Danielle asked the three magical spirits. They merely kept quiet and shrugged their shoulders.

"It looks like it is someone's garden on planet Earth," Speed Twister replied while holding the tip of his moustache.

"Oh, no! Not that place again," the Three Weird Sisters exclaimed together. Cindy clasped her arm.

***

While Speed Twister and Mother Reddy left to go to Desperate Valley, Ashley, Prince Jeff, Witchery Minister, and Bob planned to return the mystifying statues to their original selves at Trevi Fountain, ensuring peace for Pisa, the Colosseum, and Trevi Fountain.

"The three mystifying statues are on top of the leaning tower. Ashley and Witchery Minister, please lure them back to Trevi Fountain while Bob and I go search for the missing sacred eye. I need the eye for me to foresee the detailed whereabouts of the hidden last ancient sacred elements to free the Three Weird Sisters."

"Okay, please be careful, Prince Jeff and Bob," Ashley replied.

With Prince Jeff shaking his royal bracelet, his royal flying scooter appeared from the sky, and both hopped on it and flew off.

Without wasting any time, Ashley pointed her powerful sword above her head while the tip of her sword touched Witchery Minister's magic sceptre. Subsequently, a gust of wind blew past their faces, and she uttered:

Only the generation of true heart grant me with great strength.

Sprinkle with love, sprinkle with heart.

Bring us to the top of Pisa.

In a flash, both of them were standing on top of Pisa. The mystifying statues were in Pisa moving here and there; they looked confused on what to do next. Once they saw both of them, all three of them got up, and the God of the Sea lifted his Trident of Poseidon and pointed it at them.

Ashley and the Witchery Minister were quick to react. She got ready with her sword while the Witchery Minister took out his sceptre. Both released rays of cyan light towards the God of the Sea.

The Trident of Poseidon pushed against their efforts.

Ashley felt the power was strong, and her grip on her sword began slipping; therefore, she uttered, 'Bracelet, release magic shelter.'

The magic shelter covered Ashley and Witchery Minister like a transparent globe. The trident orange-red ray of light did not hit both of them. Instead, when the light hit the protective transparent globe, it ricocheted and flew back like a gun cannon that retaliated and hit the God of the Sea's left arm. His left arm was broken into pieces and fell on the ground.

Looking at the destruction that Ashley had done to his arm, his face turned red like chili. He roared and sent a signal to the other two mystifying statues. Then the three of them standing side by side released a bigger ball of an orange ray of light at Ashley and Witchery Minister.

Ashley commanded, "Magic sword, fly us to the ground of the Leaning Tower of Pisa."

With that, they vanished.

"Phew! That was close," Witchery Minister exclaimed when they reached their destination.

Once they got up from the ground, they saw three figures jumping from the top of Pisa, crushing some of the Pisa's architecture as they jumped from one level to another downwards.

"Let's get ready to face them," Ashley told Witchery Minister.

She held her sword above her waist while her digital ring released a ray of green light. It hit the mystifying statues as they came jumping from the tower.

Once the statues landed on the ground of Pisa, Witchery Minister pointed his sceptre at both the wild and docile seahorse statue. It's ray of light hit them, and they flew and rolled over a few feet away from Witchery Minister.

***

Once they arrived at Trevi Fountain, Prince Jeff and Bob were taken aback at the mess and destruction from releasing Speed Twister and activating the lives of the mystifying statues. There was a massive hole at the centre statue leaning against the wall of the Trevi Fountain, along with debris lying here and there in the fountain and beside it.

Prince Jeff activated his royal bracelet to detect the sacred eye amongst the debris and crystal-clear water flowing in the fountain. Suddenly, Bob jumped up and down excitedly. "I think I saw an eye in the water." He pointed in the right direction with some small pebbles surrounding it.

Looking at Bob being confident, Prince Jeff adjusted his searching section to the right corner, and then his royal bracelet chimed in a frenzy. Its bright light shone in the direction that Bob's paw pointed.

"Superb detective Bob." Prince Jeff was all smiles. "Come, Bob, let's go grab it."

So off they went onto the royal flying scooter and drove near to where they spotted the sacred eye. Bob was excited; he jumped down, splashing water as he swam into the fountain. It was easy for him to locate the sacred eye when Prince Jeff joined into the water since his royal auto bracelet immediately detected and drilled the remnants of pebbles to remove the sacred eye.

"Got it," Prince Jeff said.

Both jumped out from the water and hopped onto his flying scooter to land on the road nearby. Prince Jeff held the sacred eye, which released a shining ray of bright lights. Initially, the blurry vision emerged through Prince Jeff's forehead, and then a few seconds later, the vision became clear. The ancient marble silhouette appeared before their eyes, one black intertwined with silver lying on a bed of water somewhere at Trevi Fountain. Another piece that looked sapphire blue intertwined with black was hidden at the "Tugu Negara" in Kuala Lumpur.

Finally, the blood-red background with a knife picture on its centrepiece on the marble was kept safely at Ashley's grandmother's cottage.

"Bob, let's go to Ashley and Witchery Minister. We'd better get hold of the marble hidden in Ashley's grandmother's cottage before Speed Twister arrives and causes trouble."

***

Back in Desperate Valley, a silhouette of Ashley Sprinkler emerged from the crystal bowl.

"What? Why does Ashley's face appear at the cottage? Does this mean the cottage is hers?" Danielle asked the three magical spirits.

All three of them replied in chorus, "It's her grandmother's cottage."

"Revenge will start now!" Danielle, Cindy, and Angie cried out simultaneously. Danielle's hands turned to fists.

"Go, Speed Twister. Kidnap them or hurt them while Mother Reddy searches for the marble."

"My dear beautiful nieces, my, oh my, how you look ridiculously ugly when you are full of revenge. We are here not to kill Earthlings but to get hold of the sacred ancient elements to break you free, remember?" Speed Twister retorted while playing the tip of his moustache. "Mother Reddy and I are going to get hold of the three last sacred ancient items for you. Please do not do anything wicked while we both are gone. It will jeopordize your freedom."

The Three Weird Sisters nodded in agreement.

CHAPTER 20

Ashley's and Witchery Minister's sword ray of light magic hit the three mystifying statues, which caused them to be in rage and rampage the surroundings of the Pisa grounds.

Then a royal scooter appeared from one of the thick clouds; Prince Jeff and Bob passed on their findings on the whereabouts of the last three ancient sacred items and their concern for the safety of Ashley's grandmother and mother.

Ashley gasped upon hearing the location of the marble. "We need to save your grandmother and mother and relocate them to a safer place," Prince Jeff urged her. At the same time, his hands waved at her to move.

"Witchery Minister, stay here to guard the marble in black intertwined with silver located at Trevi Fountain. Please keep it safe if you can find and get it out," Prince Jeff told him.

Ashley pointed her powerful sword above their heads; subsequently, she twisted her sword back and forth and uttered:

Only the generation of true heart grant me with great strength.

Sprinkle with love, sprinkle with heart.

Let us be at my grandmother's cottage.

Poof.

All three appeared in Ashley's grandmother's cottage garden out of the blue. Its butterfly flower bushes with delphinium flowers, bougainvilleas, and hibiscus in the garden were burnt and smashed into pieces. Ashley's favorite blue swing sat collapsed on the ground surrounded by dusty sand. Holes were placed sporadically in the grass.

"Looks like Speed Twister and Mother Reddy have gone digging," Ashley said. *I hope both did not harm Grandmother and Mother*, she thought.

Bob and Ashley quickly ran into the house, standing beside the staircase, "Grandmother and Mother! Where are you?"

Her heart beat faster than usual as she feared for their safety.

Suddenly, both saw a shadow similar to Speed Twister; the shadow represented a hair shape of smashed meatballs and spaghetti. It ran past in a flash. Ashley took out her sword, getting ready to retaliate if Speed Twister attacked any of her family members.

"Dearie, where is the ancient element in the shape of a marble?"

He extended his blue hands facing Ashley's mother.

Ashley and Bob's ears twitched when both heard Speed Twister's voice coming from upstairs.

"I don't know what you're talking about," Ashley's mother answered, her voice trembling.

Ashley's grandmother replied, "Leave her alone. She doesn't know anything about magic. What are you searching for, Mr. Blue Man?"

"My name is Speed Twister. I come from the Maze Realm, not planet Earth. I believe your husband and Professor Sprinkler kept the ancient sacred marble safely somewhere in these cottage surroundings. But unfortunately, Ashley's sword cursed my nieces, the Three Weird Sisters, which trapped them in their kingdom, Desperate Valley, and I need the antidote to free them!" He stomped his feet on the floor.

Ashley heard the conversation since all three of them were talking at the landing of the staircase on the second floor. Bob made a surprise jump on Speed Twister. He opened his sharp claws and scratched Speed Twister's blue cheek, which caused Speed Twister to be taken aback. However, this was a distraction to allow Ashley some time to save her family.

While Speed Twister was repairing his injured face with his magic, Ashley flew to her mother and grandmother's side. "Bracelet, release protective magic net against Speed Twister."

A magic net glowing yellow surrounded Ashley's mother and grandmother just in time to prevent Speed Twister's magic pens from hitting and immobilizing them.

Upon seeing Ashley standing in front of him, Speed Twister quickly uttered a magic spell while he twisted and turned his two magic pens. Ashley was ready with her magic sword pointing at his chest, and her magical auto ring released a ray of green light that hit one of Speed Twister's magic pens. The ray of light burnt the side of his hand.

"Ouch, you naughty Ashley!" He quickly jumped down the staircase, landed safely on the ground, and muttered a spell, and his magic pen flew from upstairs into his hand.

Ashley tried to catch him by jumping downstairs. Once she descended, Speed Twister jumped upstairs and then scurried to her dad's study room. Once he stepped inside, he could feel good magic amongst his skin, which made goosebumps appear. He stood opposite a straight-backed comfortable wooden chair and an antique writing table in mahogany brown.

Then his magic pen moved in a circle twice before it tipped; the pen stopped and pointed at the direction of a Persian carpet with a peacock design. The location was on the floor next to the antique table. Speed Twister's eyes wandered here and there on the carpet, then on the wooden floor, but he could not find any ancient sacred items in a shape of a marble. His magic pen insisted that the item was hidden within the carpet. Feeling exasperated to get hold of it soon, he uttered some spells. Finally, his eyes detected the eye of the peacock, embedded in the carpet thread, was the ancient sacred item in a shape of a marble. "This is the item I am looking for." He smiled and clapped his hands once.

As he was about to kneel and get closer to look at it, he heard Ashley kicking the door. Then he heard her auto ring drilling the locked doorknob. As Speed Twister turned his head to face the carpet, his mouth opened widely, and then he said, "Got it. Professor Sprinkler, you are cunning."

Then, the door sprung open with Ashley holding her sword facing at Speed Twister. He instantly tore the carpet at the peacock eyes design. Then he grabbed the marble with a blood red background with a knife picture as it protruded from the carpet, just in time before Ashley's auto ring shone a green light on his shoe to release some smoke. However, it did not deter him from running away. With his magic pen, his legs carried him through the thick wall of the study room, and he jumped onto Mother Reddy's fluffy feathers. To Ashley's surprise, Mother Reddy was flapping her wings just outside the invisible study wall.

"So long, naughty Ashley!" Speed Twister shouted.

Ashley ran and jumped to catch Speed Twister. As she pointed her sword at Speed Twister, the ray of light hit a wall.

Speed Twister's magic dissipated since he was gone; therefore, she could not go through the walls, nor were her rays of light able to hit Speed Twister.

Ashley was still running towards Speed Twister when she hit her face on the wall. "Ouch!"

She blinked her eyes in disbelief that a blank wall surrounded the study room, and she could neither see nor chase after Speed Twister. So, Ashley was left alone, with Prince Jeff following behind her.

The door to the study room sprung opened, and her grandmother and mother appeared. Both were speechless upon seeing the torn Persian carpet on the floor and a young man dressed like a prince standing beside Ashley.

"Grandmother and Mother, this is Prince Jeff from the Goodness Realm. He is my good friend in my adventure to other realms along with Bob, Billy, and Dash. I used the sword and magic artifacts that Father left for my adventures," Ashley said to them, pointing her index finger towards Prince Jeff.

Her grandmother and mother hugged her. "Thank you for saving us," Grandmother said while kissing her forehead.

"It was a dreadful experience. Please be careful in this adventure against evil creatures," Mother expressed with her forehead puckered.

"Excuse us, we better run along to get hold of the last ancient sacred marbles at "Tugu Negara" and Rome. But don't worry, I will protect Ashley," Prince Jeff said, concurrently curtsy.

With that, Ashley pointed her powerful sword towards the ceiling, and then she twisted her sword back and forth and uttered:

Only the generation of true heart grant me with great strength.

Sprinkle with love, sprinkle with heart.

Let us be at "Tugu Negara."

The three of them vanished into thin air, leaving her family surprised.

***

While Ashley explained and introduced Prince Jeff to her grandmother and mother, Mother Reddy flew past Parliament at Kuala Lumpur, Malaysia. They soon arrived at the Perdana Botanical Garden.

Drivers in their transportation were alarmed by the darkness covering their sky when Mother Reddy passed by. Some stopped their cars or motorcycles to catch a glimpse of the enormous bird.

"We are nearing; please slow down, Mother Reddy," Speed Twister advised her.

She slowed her wings, descending and reducing their speed.

Then beautiful stairways stood majestically before the monument of "Tugu Negara," a statue consisting of seven soldiers carrying the Malaysian flag resembling seven qualities of leadership (remembrance of the fallen soldiers during the fight for freedom to independence in Malaysia).

Mother Reddy saw the tip of the "Tugu Negara," passed a fountain and blue tiles, and then descended and landed.

All visitors standing near the stairway a few metres from the "Tugu Negara" gasped and started screaming once they saw Mother Reddy, the enormous bird, and a man with his hair in a shape of smashed meatballs in Bolognese colour on his head with blue skin. His green eyes glared at them, which made some scream as he passed by.

Speed Twister turned a blind eye to those visitors'actions and jumped down from Mother Reddy's body. Then he held two of his shiny magic pens above his chest and twisted and turned his wrists to turn both pens clockwise.

The ancient teeth and nails from both the kangaroo and koala kept in his pocket started squirming. And then they pushed his pocket widely, popping out in front of Speed Twister at eye level.

Magic dust sprinkled amongst the items as they stood still in front of Speed Twister overlooking the "Tugu Negara" monument.

"Ancient sacred elements, reveal to me the marble decorated with sapphire blue background intertwined with black colour in its centrepiece."

Blinking and clamouring started to emanate from the sacred items, and then the statue made from bronze, one of the statues holding a Malaysia flag, began to move and looked lively at Speed Twister.

"Why did you wake me up?" The statue turned his face and spoke face to face with Speed Twister.

"According to our knowledge, we are searching for the ancient sacred marble that is kept within your statue." Speed Twister pointed at the statue's body.

"Look no further. The item you seek is in the statue to my left. It is hidden at the tip of his long gun." Then the statue closed his eyes and returned to his original statue self.

Thereafter, Speed Twister hastened his steps from his spot of one metre away from the "Tugu Negara" monument. In a flash, he jumped onto the "Tugu Negara" and landed on its platform, since his height was similar to the statue, then scurried to the side of the soldier holding a long rifle. He touched the tip of the gun. Since the ancient sacred from Sydney magic power was still in the air surrounding the statue, Speed Twister's pointed fingers magically were able to slide into the tip of the rifle. It slid in until it reached the middle of the rifle, and then he felt a complex item in a circular shape. He smiled to himself. *I finally got it.*

The marble rolled over into his hands; he pulled his long, skinny arms out slowly from the old rifle made of bronze.

Immediately, he jumped down from the monument, and then he waved at the sacred items found from Sydney, which were still floating in the air, to return to his pocket.

"Let's go to Trevi Fountain." Speed Twister patted Mother Reddy's neck.

Once Mother Reddy was getting ready to fly off, Ashley and Prince Jeff arrived a few metres from the place that Mother Reddy and Speed Twister were standing.

Speed Twister waved his hands menacingly at them. "I got it first, naughty Ashley." Unfortunately, the marble was shining against the sunlight, which blinded Ashley and Prince Jeff.

Speed Twister raised his two magical pens and said a magic spell.

Poof.

They were gone.

Seeing them vanish, without wasting any time, Ashley pointed her powerful sword toward the sky, and then she twisted her sword back and forth and uttered:

Only the generation of true heart grant me with great strength.

Sprinkle with love, sprinkle with heart.

Let us be at Trevi Fountain.

The three of them vanished.

***

The last ancient sacred element was hidden at the Trevi Fountain.

Prince Jeff entrusted Witchery Minister to search for the item while he and Ashley saved Ashley's grandmother and mother in Kuala Lumpur.

Witchery Minister used his long sceptre to locate the last sacred item; it was believed to be a marble with design in black intertwined with silver. The item was supposed to be hidden in the water at Trevi Fountain. He shifted the pebbles one by one to search for the sacred items to no avail. He did not possess the magic to identify and see things.

"Hi, old man. Looking tired after an extensive search." Speed Twister appeared and sneered at Witchery Minister.

Witchery Minister turned his head, looking at Speed Twister.

Speed Twister uttered a spell while twisting and turning his magic pens, which released a ray of red light towards Witchery Minister's direction. He was so taken aback by the sudden appearance of Speed Twister that he only managed to shift his magic sceptre located at his side towards his centre. Although Witchery Minister was not fast enough to prevent the ray of red light from hitting him, he managed to jump into the fountain due to the severity of the evil magic hitting his sceptre and stomach. He crouched in pain in the water.

Without any delay, Speed Twister pulled out the two sacred marbles from his magic pouch, which wriggled and shuddered as he held them in his palm. Then the two magic marbles floated in the air at the same level as Speed Twister's eyes with a sprinkle of magic dust dancing among them. A bright, magical light blinded the eyes of Speed Twister when the two sacred elements shone in the opposite direction of Trevi Fountain. It showed the silhouette of the marble located at a souvenir shop named Trevi Gallery.

"The last marble is hidden in that shop?" Speed Twister quickly got up from the fountain's steps and ran in haste towards the souvenir shop.

"Move aside!" he shouted while his blue hands pushed passers-by. Since he was in a hurry, he tripped and brushed shoulders against visitors as he went.

Once he arrived at the shop, he panted and inhaled the air deeply to regain his composure. Many around him were perturbed by his appearance.

"Why are you staring at me?" Speed Twister uttered a spell, making everyone freeze. "That is better. Humans are weird."

The two marbles were menacing, knocking at each other as though they were dancing and then shuddering strongly above a transparent glass showcase. Then, like a torchlight, both marbles shone a bright light on a mask laid in the centre of the glass showcase.

Speed Twister smiled to himself. "Finally, I will find the cure for my nieces, and we can rule the entire universe."

His ears started to twitch when he heard a little girl's voice. His magic pen started to vibrate. "Why are you acting weird, my magic pen?" Next, he placed his skinny blue fingers on both sides of his head, providing him a silhouette of Ashley. "Aha! Ashley and her team have arrived. She will not stop me this time. I better hurry."

His long, skinny hands grabbed hold of a Venetian Carnival mask in glittering red and black. Its forehead had a stone decorated with red feathers; it was a marble in black intertwined with silver. "It is all mine."

He ran out from the shop at top speed, leaving behind frozen humans. He bumped into Ashley, but he pushed her aside with his magic hands.

With his forceful push, Ashley stumbled backwards. He ran a few metres forward, and in between running, he turned to look at Ashley's distance to his. But he could not see her anywhere.

"Mother Reddy, where are you? Please be quick to save me!" Speed Twister shouted. Then, as he turned his head facing north, he saw Mother Reddy standing sturdy with her wings flapping. He scurried and jumped on Mother Reddy's strong feathers, and they flew away.

***

Prince Jeff grabbed Ashley's shoulders, "Let Speed Twister go. We must save the humans, recuperate, and restore Trevi Fountain to normal. We will fight with him and the Three Weird Sisters when the time comes."

Thereafter, both using their magic swords and uttering some spells, humans were returned to normal, and they celebrated. Ashley activated her auto magic bracelet facing the Trevi Fountain to restore the beautifully decorated stones of Trevi Fountain. Having healing power, she touched the stomach of Witchery Minister, and his injury recovered within a few minutes.

"According to my senses magic that I activated using my royal auto bracelet, the mystifying statues are no longer in Rome," Prince Jeff said.

Ashley agreed, "I can feel in my bones that those three are under Speed Twister's control as long as he has the ancient sacred items from Sydney. We will eventually restore them."

CHAPTER 21

Thud.

Mother Reddy made some noises as she landed hurriedly on the messy ground of the mansion of Desperate Valley Realm.

Speed Twister jumped down from her feathered wings, smoothing his jacket and shaking off dust. Then he twisted and turned one of his magic pens and muttered a spell; he appeared magically in front of his nieces at their administrative room.

"My nieces, I have good news; here are the three last ancient sacred items found." He opened his palm to reveal those items.

"Good job, Uncle, we will be freed in a jiffy and resume our conquest!" Danielle responded with a grin.

"Let me start the ritual," Speed Twister suggested.

With his skinny fingers holding two of his magic pens, he twisted and turned his wrists. All four ancient sacred items were placed one by one and side by side into the crystal bowl located on a table. Subsequently, all four of them circled the crystal bowl, walked at the rhythm of the merry-go-round three times, and then smoke appeared. Next, their chandelier started flickering and chiming.

Firstly, the dragon's skin, now red, appeared. Ms. Pontianak, Bunyip, and a three-headed monster with its skin texture like a toad in mud colour appeared amongst the smoke.

"Why do you summon us?" the spirits asked.

Ms. Pontianak's red eyes glared at Speed Twister's eyes.

"We beseech you to release the curse befallen upon the Three Weird Sisters," Speed Twister replied.

"Let us hold all three heads to feel the intensity of the curse."

The four magical spirits held the Three Weird Sisters' heads; all four of their bodies shuddered and ended with sweat dripping.

"It is a good-hearted curse; you need to sacrifice a breathing being for you to be free from this curse."

"What about the cake lady? Yes, we can sacrifice her," Cindy suggested.

"In addition to that, we also require you to trap the cursed spirit into something so that it will not release and haunt you ladies."

"The butterfly Swarovski would be a good place to hide this cursed spirit. No one will have any clue," Angie responded.

Once Speed Twister flickered his long, skinny fingers, the cake lady appeared before their eyes. Danielle pointed her fingers towards the cake lady, and she grew back into her original human size.

"Please, let me go." The cake lady clasped her hands.

Angie mimicked the cake lady's tone of pleading. "Yes, of course." Angie twisted and turned her right hand with her mouth, muttering a spell.

Then the four ancient magical spirits surrounded the cake lady. They chanted and walked at clockwise direction for four times. Their action developed a small whirlwind around the cake lady, who was screaming; her hands were wailing here and there, trying to grab hold onto something to release herself.

"Help! Help!" Next, in a heartbeat, her soul came out from her body, and then the four magical spirits took turns swallowing her soul. Then the four spirits spit the new magic on the Three Weird Sisters, who were in a circle beside them. The ancient magic, plus human soul twirling with magic dust, lightning, and thunder, circled the Three Weird Sisters. This caused them to float in the air at the same height as the crystal bowl. All three of them shone brightly.

"Argh! Argh!" The Three Weird Sisters shouted in pain as the powerful magic entered firstly from their heads to their toes. It was painful since the powerful, ancient magic was fighting with the good-hearted curse to neutralize the curse within their bodies.

Once the curse and the powerful sacred spirits fought with each other and ended, the Three Weird Sisters vomited a greenish liquid into a Swarovski's butterfly pendant shape. The Swarovski shone and shuddered as the curse and human soul entered and settled.

This activity caused the Three Weird Sisters to be drenched in sweat.

"I will be wearing the butterfly Swarovski; no one can come close to it," Danielle spoke.

"Can the curse be gone forever without keeping it safe in an item?" Angie looked at the four magical spirits while asking.

"It will be gone once it meets with Ashley's good-hearted sword," the four magical spirits replied together.

"Ashley, I soon will meet you to end this misery," Angie swore.

"With the successful ritual, we will return to sleep." All four spirits bent their heads with respect for the Three Weird Sisters, then absorbed into their own individual ancient sacred items in a flash.

Danielle smiled. "We will begin our conquest."

CHAPTER 22

"What are we waiting for?" Danielle said while chuckling to her sisters and Speed Twister. They were busy discussing at the administrative room of Desperate Valley.

Henceforth, with snapping their skinny fingers three times, then walking in a circle facing clockwise three times, they held hands while raising their arms high up and uttered a few spells. Thick, greyish smoke with a sprinkle of magic dust appeared, encircling them.

Seeing this, refusing to be left behind from the conquest to govern the Scarlet Zamrud Realm, Speed Twister quickly jumped and joined the sisters in the blink of an eye.

Poof.

***

The four of them were confident that their evil magic could easily bring them straight to the Scarlet Zamrud Realm. Once they reached the entrance of the realm, to their utter dismay, they could not see anything. "According to my magic compass, the realm is at the spot we are standing," Angie said, checking her compass.

"Let me use my power!" Danielle placed her skinny fingers on the sides of her forehead, and then her eyes opened widely.

"What did you see?" Angie asked.

"The realm is just a few steps from where we are standing. Let's go," Danielle said.

All four of them stepped closer to the designated spot. Once their feet touched the entrance, an electric current emerged and strangled their legs. The impact was massive and caused them to flip backwards.

"Argh! Unbelievable. Our evil magic was unable to penetrate the entrance," Danielle said. 'Speed Twister, what shall we do?'

"Remember, I told you that we must have several plans, so let us follow my second plan. That is to contact and bribe Witch Z's Head of Underworld of Zamrud Realm. He is my long-lost cousin, outcasted from Maze Realm for stealing and betrayal," Speed Twister suggested. Underworld was located just beside Zamrud Realm; therefore, anyone could go in and out easily. "Wait for me here, my nieces."

In the blink of an eye, Speed Twister was gone.

He appeared before his cousin Albertor at the Underworld.

"Hello. It's me, your beloved cousin."

Chief Albertor dropped a pen that he was holding and grinned upon seeing his relative. "What can I do for you, cousin?"

"I know you loathe Witch Z as much as I do. Let's rule the Scarlet Zamrud Realm," Speed Twister suggested. "In order to do so, how can you help a non-citizen like me and my nieces to enter Zamrud Realm? I promised you that you will be the next Prime Minister once we conquer this realm."

"That is a good opportunity, but I also require some money too. I have a pile of debts.'

"Sure, whatever you want. Your wish is my command," Speed Twister replied.

CHAPTER 23

Speed Twister informed the Three Weird Sisters of the good news that his cousin would assist them in entering the Zamrud Realm.

"Let's go!" Danielle exclaimed excitedly.

They were to go through a secret passage via the Underworld. It was located at the edge just beside Zamrud Realm, underneath its grounds and situated on a dark side where dead creatures were buried and evil creatures were tortured in misty and smelly dungeons.

Once they reached the Underworld, Albertor stood sturdy at the entrance, welcoming Speed Twister and the Three Weird Sisters. He placed a small pouch on Speed Twister's palm. Both looked at each other, and Speed Twister nodded.

The four of them walked until the edge of the Underworld and Speed Twister held the pouch above their heads.

Poof.

"Argh! Unbelievable. I smell like dog urine," Danielle grumbled.

"And spotted green slime stuck on my pants!" Angie shouted. This incident happened when they mysteriously appeared via one of the unkept graveyards at Zamrud Realm through a secret passageway from the Underworld.

"What do you expect from evil creatures like us? So, we are at the back door entrance of Zamrud Realm. I managed to make a deal to obtain the stone spell from one Witch Z traitor. Otherwise, we could never have reached this realm alive," Speed Twister responded.

***

At her administrative chamber, Witch Z's magic mirror shook abruptly, and then it exploded into pieces of broken glass. Upon seeing the tragic behaviour of her magic mirror, Witch Z retraced her steps and said, "Mirror, my friend, what did you see and fear?'

In the blink of an eye, the many broken glass pieces that floated in the air fixed instantly magically. Then the mirror showed the faces of the Three Weird Sisters and Speed Twister.

"I wonder what they want in such a haste."

Witch Z snapped her fingers, and her sceptre flew into her hands. The sceptre was designed as the head of a dragon, its eyes blaring ruby-red.

"Let's welcome our wicked uninvited guests." She smiled.

The dragon on her sceptre roared in agreement.

***

The Three Weird Sisters and Speed Twister walked further away from the graveyard. They entered the southern region of Zamrud Realm. "Listen to me. I am your new leader." They spoke to the Zamrud Realm citizens when they were eye to eye. Next, Danielle uttered a spell while her skinny fingers released evil magic in a ray of red light and threw in the air a magic pebble that the Witch Z traitor gave to them in the Underworld.

The evil magic combined with Speed Twister's evil magic caused the magic pebbles to burst into fireworks. Their magic spread all over the south region of Zamrud Realm and made all the citizens spellbound.

All of their faces turned to a Tata Duende lookalike; they were 92 cm tall and had pointy faces, flat noses, and hooded red eyes. However, the variety of hat colours differentiated them. Originally Tata Duende were Desperate Valley Realm's security team. "We are at your command," they chanted. "You are our queen, our leader, Danielle!"

***

Witch Z's mirror shook and made a lot of noises. "Your Majesty, I have bad news. Please look at the centre of me, Your Majesty. My magic detected intrusion by the Three Weird Sisters and Speed Twister. As you can view from my centrepiece glass, the south region of Scarlet Zamrud citizens were turned to Tata Duende by their evil magic. Furthermore, they are embracing The Three Weird Sisters as their new leaders."

The magic mirror continued to show the location and the expanse of the evil conquest. Witch Z's palm smacked on her forehead, and she gasped when she saw the map of Zamrud Realm. It indicated electronically that 30 percent of her kingdom was under Three Weird Sisters' control. They were no longer happy as before.

Quickly thinking to save what was left of her kingdom, she tapped her magic sceptre on her castle floor twice. Then her castle and its grounds were encircled with magic protection in a transparent globe.

Her red ruby necklace started glowing when she closed her eyes, as well as holding her magic sceptre. She concentrated on contacting the Goodness Realm for help.

CHAPTER 24

While Ashley and Prince Jeff were concentrating on cleaning and putting Trevi Fountain back to its original surroundings, his royal auto bracelet started to move frantically to and fro on his wrist. His magical royal belt began to shudder.

"Oh my, what is happening?" Prince Jeff yelled out in surprise.

Suddenly, his belt released a silhouette figure of Witch Z. Her brows were furrowed, and her eyes looked at him intently.

"My dear nephew, I need help; my magic alone cannot defeat The Three Weird Sisters and Speed Twister. They are here invading. I am not sure how they can enter Zamrud Realm. Their evil magic is limited to gaining access to Zamrud Realm. I supposed there is a Zamrud Realm citizen that helped them." Her voice cracked as the communication died.

Ashley and Prince Jeff looked at each other.

"Amazing, through my knowledge, only those creatures with blood relation with the Scarlet Zamrud Realm can enter easily. I wonder who has assisted those evil, greedy witches," Prince Jeff said.

Prince Jeff faced Ashley with a half smile. "I need to bring you in this battle. We need your sword magic to defeat those four witches."

"From my knowledge from learning the magic, witchcraft, and technologies at Goodness Realm University, in order to restore Zamrud Realm that has fallen onto evil witches, we must have the combination of good magic from three different areas and different items. That will be Witch Z's sceptre from Zamrud Realm, your sword from Earth, and my sword from the Goodness Realm," he added.

Ashley nodded.

"Why are they interested in ruling the Scarlet Zamrud Realm?" Ashley asked while placing her right index finger under her chin.

"It is known that any creatures who own Zamrud Realms and the artifacts, like Witch Z's scepter and powerful ruby necklace, will be powerful enough to rule the entire universe, realms, and Earth." Prince Jeff provided the information.

"In addition, they can control and demolish the entire universe once they capture Scarlet Zamrud Realm," Prince Jeff continued. His forehead crease was visible this time.

"That is not going to happen. I will not let them," Ashley said firmly with a fist on her left hand.

***

Witch Z and her loyal subjects flew on an auto flying vehicle shaped like a bird to the centre, east, and west of her kingdom. Once she arrived in each section of her realm, she jumped down, remained afloat in the air of each region, raised her golden hands, snapped her right fingers twice, and then raised her magic sceptre high above the skyline and uttered a spell. A protective transparent globe fenced the skyline of the centre region.

Next, she and her loyal subjects flew to the eastern region. She breathed deeply and smiled, seeing the wicked witches still unenthralled here. Witch Z snapped her golden fingers while she raised her magic sceptre high above the skyline to utter a spell. Her eyes opened widely upon witnessing several thick clouds moving fast towards the eastern region. From her mid-air spot, she could view the edge of the region gradually covered by muddy green liquid. She noticed that the magic green liquid transformed her citizens one by one into Tata Duende's appearance once it touched them. Then the gardens with beautiful roses, orchids, purple coral bells, and blue star flowers turned to crabgrasses with pots of mud here and there with flies flying when the liquid spread on them.

"We are too late; we only managed to protect my castle grounds and the northern regions." Witch Z wrapped her hands around herself; gradually, the colour of her cheeks went white.

"Witch Z, watch out!" One of her loyal subjects took out her sword and hit the greenish liquid away from Witch Z. In an instant, Witch Z raised her sceptre, and all her subjects returned to her castle grounds.

She breathed deeply, her hands clenching into fists. "My magic mirror, who assisted the witches in entering my kingdom?"

Her mirror started blinking, and then a tiny gulf of smoke emerged with the face of Chief Albertor. Then the mirror wrote on the glass: "The Traitor." The mirror shared his background.

"No wonder. He was an escaped convict who, due to my mercy, agreed to accept his regret, and now I am enduring his revenge." Witch Z tightened her jaw.

The castle grounds were situated next to the western region that had been conquered by the four witches, and screaming and shrieking noises emanated from that direction.

"I guess the malice has spread rapidly and will enter my castle grounds any minute. All soldiers are on guard for a war!" Witch Z shouted. *This is the first time under my leadership I was betrayed.*

She clenched her teeth.

Snapping her golden fingers brought her to the edge of her castle grounds, along with her subjects and soldiers. Just in time, it seemed, as the Three Weird Sisters and Speed Twister arrived outside the magic protective shield.

"What do you want from my kingdom?"

"We want to be their leaders and control the whole universe," replied Danielle with a laugh, and then she nodded to Speed Twister.

He threw the ancient sacred elements from Sydney in the air and uttered a spell with two of his magic pens facing the sacred items. The three mystifying statues from the Trevi Fountain appeared, roaring, face to face with Witch Z and her entourage. The three of them huffed and puffed, pushing against the protective wall, but an electric current emerged from the wall and threw them off, making them tumble on the muddy grasses.

Danielle clapped her hands, and then Angie, Cindy, and Speed Twister stood side by side, raised their hands high up, and turned their palms towards the protective wall. A ray of red light emerged, burning the layer of the wall. Their evil magic pushed, strongly hitting the protective wall, which was undeterred. The evil magic died in a few minutes; however, due to the frequency of the evil magic hitting the protective wall, it was dented, and its layers gradually thinned.

Upon seeing the intensity of the evil witch's magic penetrating bit by bit the protective wall, Witch Z touched her red ruby necklace. This action released a ray of red plus a black ray of magic power light with a sprinkle of magic dust, hitting the wall where the evil witches were standing to create another protective layer.

She said, "I will not allow my castle grounds and entourage to be held captive."

A silhouette of a creature could be seen inch bit by bit walking towards the four witches. Soon, the creature reached the border of the protective wall; it was clearly Chief Albertor. Once he stood just beside the protective wall, he raised his arrow and bow. He shot several magic marbles onto the protective wall.

The magic marble from the Scarlet Zamrud Realm penetrated the protective transparent wall. As a result, the protective wall opened like the zipper of a bag.

Witch Z quickly raised her sceptre, pointing it towards the protective wall cracks to recreate the protective globe. Her loyal security standing tall beside her were equipped with shields, swords, and laser guns. They were prepared to fight the evil witches once the protective shield was broken.

Thereafter, Three Weird Sisters, Speed Twister, Mother Reddy, the three mystifying statues, and Chief Albertor stood side by side, using their evil magic to push against Witch Z's magic sceptre. Nine against one, Witch Z could not withhold against the evil powers. She snapped her golden fingers; red and black lights intertwined, and then they hit the cracks of the broken protective wall, burning Mother Reddy's left-wing feathers. Finally, she left the witch's circle, weakening the evil magic ray of lights.

Now, it is eight against one, I have better chances to win this battle, Witch Z thought to herself.

The mystifying statues were furious, moving on their spot, and roared. Once they saw the cracks fit for them, they slid into the castle grounds.

The ground gave way to cracks, then holes, which the ten royal soldiers standing nearby fell into.

Upon witnessing some of her soldiers being defeated by the evil witches, Witch Z turned her sceptre to focus on assisting with her entourage's safety. But unfortunately, with the change of plans, the protective wall was broken by the evil power of the greedy witches and Zamrud Realm's traitor, Chief Albertor.

Her magic sceptre released a red and black intertwined ray of magic light that hit the mystifying statue, which led them to be burnt and frozen to the spot.

The Three Weird Sisters with Speed Twister chanted their evil spells and raised their hands in a circle. This created a gust of strong wind coupled with a tornado. The castle grounds were damaged with uprooted plants and defoliated triangle-shaped pine trees. A strong evil wind blew, causing the soldiers one by one to be thrown away into the evil tornado.

"Argh, help me!" one of the soldiers cried out as her legs were unable to withhold the strong current. Suddenly, she felt a strong grip pull her away. As she turned, she saw a young girl equipped with a sword, pointing her finger, which had an auto ring, towards her body. A magic rope clutched her waist and pulled her to safety hidden behind a concrete wall just beside the entrance of Witch Z's castle.

"Witch Z, now bow to me and accept your defeat!" Danielle shrieked with her eyes glowing red, looking at Witch Z. Both of her hands twisted and turned to create a ball of evil fire. Witch Z managed to signal at Ashley not to fight yet. Ashley hid herself behind three bushes of lush greenery, getting ready to save Witch Z when her time came.

The Three Weird Sisters twisted their wrists and then the ball of evil fire shot directly at Witch Z. She retaliated by flickering her golden fingers with a strong blow, leaving

Danielle to flip and fall over. She immediately got up, and Speed Twister signalled at her. Then she released her evil ray of red light combined with Speed Twister's magic pen. This powerful combination hit Witch Z in her heart, leaving her to fall apart like a dissipated piece of broken glass.

"Ha ha ha! I finally won." Danielle laughed.

To her amazement, the broken glass pieces danced in the air, moving hastily before blowing in her face. A glass cut appeared on her left cheek, and she was bleeding. Then the dancing glasses combined to form Witch Z's body. She stood sturdy, holding her sceptre a few metres from the castle entrance. She smiled, looking at Danielle.

"Argh, I have been fooled," Danielle cried out; she felt a burning sensation inside her heart. Then her eyes released a ray of red fluorescent light, which blew towards Witch Z.

Ashley's good-hearted sword, which had additional gems at its pommel, worked like a mirror; the red fluorescent magic light bounced back towards Danielle, burning one of her fingers.

"Ashley, you came in the nick of time to save us," Witch Z told her with a smile.

Ashley walked towards the cracks of the protection wall, swayed her sword, and uttered a magic spell. A ray of a magic blue light covered her surroundings; with a swing of her sword, the Three Weird Sisters and Speed Twister were thrown away.

Chief Albertor threw the magic marble onto Ashley's face to blind her vision; however, her auto ring released a face shield that caused the magic to splat onto the shield.

Next, Mother Reddy flew rapidly, opening her claws to scratch Ashley's face. However, her auto ring released a PVC net that caused her claws to get stuck.

With a swing of her sword, Ashley managed to release a ray of magic light onto Mother Reddy's leg, burning some of her claws. Finally, she flapped her wings vigorously, breaking free from the PVC net.

Ashley ran forward to face the three mystifying statues. With the sword in her hand, she swung and hit the mystifying statues' necks. All three of them broke into pieces.

While Ashley was busy fighting and defending, the Three Weird Sisters, Speed Twister, and Chief Alberto used their evil magic spells with a mixture of magic pebbles as they commanded, "All Tata Duende, grow your roots and glide."

Instantly, all Tata Duende grew roots like trees and glided towards the castle. Their movements were as fast as lightning. Once they approached the castle, one quietly snapped onto Ashley's leg; then, another gripped her waist. Roots surrounded Witch Z, squeezing her tightly around her neck, causing her to be unable to breathe. The roots covered with thorns cuffed her golden hands with spikes. The strong grip caused Witch Z to let go of her magic sceptre.

Seeing this, Danielle squeezed her hands and raised her arms in the air. "Magic sceptre of Scarlet Zamrud, I am your new queen. Please come to me!" The magic sceptre flew towards Danielle.

Ashley, upon witnessing this, said a magic spell: "Bracelet, release steel shield." Suddenly, a steel shield appeared before the sceptre. It hit the steel shield and flipped away from Danielle's hands. Then, her auto ring hid the sceptre.

Poof. The sceptre was gone.

"Argh!" Danielle shouted, baring her teeth and pointing her hand towards the roots of the tree. She uttered a spell that left the roots to grow spikes. It moved fast and squeezed Ashley's leg.

She tried to escape from the strong grip of the roots to no avail. After struggling a few minutes, luck was with her. In her struggle, the roots' grip loosened to release a small gap, and her auto magical ring and bracelet were no longer held. She said a spell, "Bracelet, chop off the roots." It cut off the roots into tiny pieces that freed her. The roots reproduced immediately and moved rapidly to grab Ashley's leg. Seeing their hurried movements, Ashley uttered a spell to freeze them.

While Ashley concentrated on releasing herself, the Three Weird Sisters and Speed Twister managed to turn Witch Z into a statue made from Carrara marble with their magical pens and fingers.

Danielle commented, "That should do the trick." Then, with the help of Chief Albertor, Danielle, Cindy, and Angie entered the castle grounds.

CHAPTER 25

The Three Weird Sisters snapped their magic evil fingers twice, and they turned their bodies 365 degrees. This action made Zamrud Realm's castle walls surrounded by mud and long grass with insects flying hither and thither.

Ashley gasped at the sight of this. Someone grabbed her arms. She turned to look and sighed. "What a relief! It's you, Prince Jeff. Let's save the castle."

Ashley and Prince Jeff's swords touched each other and emitted a ray of lights that moved fast and hit the castle grounds. The ray of magic lights hit and pushed the evil magic on the ground that then dissipated into thin air. Both stepped forward with the help of Ashley's magic shield from her bracelet; she managed to prevent both of them from being covered by Danielle's evil spell.

The Three Weird Sisters and Speed Twister stood sturdy at the castle entrance, ready with their magic powers; the evil power ran at top speed, and as it was about to hit Ashley and Prince Jeff, it instead hit their swords and dissipated like a speck of dust.

Witnessing the weakness in their magic power, the Three Weird Sisters and Speed Twister curled their lips while their eyes rolled. A gust of wind formed a tornado. Then the Three Weird Sisters, with their arms, pushed the tornado towards Ashley and Prince Jeff.

"Bracelet, release turbine-sucking machine." Ashley's auto ring activated the turbine. The machine sucked the tornado into its direction and then vanished.

The four of them looked at each other and gulped.

The four witches crept to leave the castle grounds, knowing that they had been defeated with their powers unable to protect Zamrud Realm castle from Ashley and Prince Jeff's goodhearted power.

"Where do you think you're going, evil witches?" Ashley talked loudly while her magic sword faced them.

They turned around to face Ashley. They vanished when Speed Twister threw a magic marble in the air above their heads while the Three Weird Sisters snapped their fingers.

"Guess they chickened out," Prince Jeff said with a chuckle.

However, the four witches were unlucky. In order to return to Desperate Valley, they required more magic marbles upon reaching the sky to escape from Zamrud Realm atmosphere. They utilised all the marbles they had; therefore, they were stuck hanging at the atmosphere.

Bang. Bang. "Ouch! My head! There are some hard forces pushing us down in this Zamrud Realm sky. Why can't we fly away from this realm?" Angie asked.

"We need the magic marble to release us," Speed Twister replied.

Next, his fingers randomly trying to find marbles in his two pockets.

"Do you have any spares?"

Ashley pointed her powerful sword toward the Witch Z statue's direction. She twisted her sword back and forth and uttered:

Only the generation of true heart grant me with great strength.

Sprinkle with love, sprinkle with heart.

Disperse the evil spell.

Within a few seconds, Witch Z returned to her usual self.

Then they heard a loud shrieking above their heads overlooking the sky, seeing four silhouettes. "It must be the Three Weird Sisters and Speed Twister. They must be stuck at my kingdom's territory. No one can return without my permission or the magic marble," Witch Z said. "Let's teach them a lesson and keep them there temporarily. We will release them once my kingdom is back in place."

Ashley and Prince Jeff smiled at her suggestion.

Witch Z told Ashley and Prince Jeff, "Let's restore the kingdom."

With her sword, Ashley flew to the south while she was still in the air; she swayed her magic sword and uttered the words:

Only the generation of true heart grant me with great strength.

Sprinkle with love, sprinkle with heart.

Return this kingdom to normal.

Soon after, those citizens' features, similar to Tata Duende, changed to normal. The long, muddy weeds covered with flies turned bit by bit to butterfly peas bushes with delphinium. Then, the stormy and gloomy clouds dispersed, replaced by sun and rainbows. A variety of birds starting to sing a happy song.

"Thank you, Ashley and Prince Jeff, for restoring my kingdom."

Ashley nodded, then twisted her sword, which caused a sunny ray of light to emerge above her head. But then Chief Albertor faced Witch Z.

Chief Albertor threw the magic marbles and his sharp dagger onto Witch Z. They fell a step away from Witch Z's feet since Ashley's sword managed to be a shield.

Not agreeing to defeat, Chief Albertor threw a few magic pebbles, this time in red colour, towards Witch Z's face. Fortunately for Witch Z, Ashley's sword was fast to hit like a baseball bat. Due to the sword's impact, the magic pebbles retaliated and hit Chief Albertor. It blinded him with smoke.

"Argh! My eyes are burning!" he cried.

"You are a traitor, Chief Albertor. Therefore, I will strip your position and title for your disgraceful act of treason. You will be burnt in the scariest dungeon."

Albertor next found himself in a pitch-dark, smelly dungeon. It held many skulls with stale blood splattered on the walls and floor. In the corner of the dungeon, Albertor could see a huge dark emerald-green dragon. Its eyes were opened widely while its long tongue dripped with saliva.

Albertor came at the right time for its lunchtime, and he quickly became the dragon's meal.

***

"Argh! Please free us, Witch Z. We promise not to conquer your kingdom again!" Danielle shouted from her spot in the sky.

"Well, LalockLalock Bibilock." Witch Z twisted and turned her golden magic fingers along with her sceptre, pointing at the four evil greedy witches.

Poof.

Once they returned to Desperate Valley, a dark emerald-green dragon with sharp teeth started chasing after them in their gardens. It had the Scarlet Zamrud Realm emblem indicated on its scutes. "I will get you for this, Witch Z!" screamed the Three Weird Sisters while running to save themselves.

ABOUT THE AUTHOR

Sherlina Idid studied in Coventry University, United Kingdom and graduated with a BA Hons in International Relations & Politics. She has been working in the human resource management line.

Her interest in traveling has led her to be exposed to other cultures, environments, and sightseeing which eventually sparked her to write her first novel *Mystical Adventure of Ashley Sprinkler (Book Series)*. Eventually her interest in writing expanded from middle grade fantasy into psychological thriller and thriller genre. She can be reached on @sherlinaididauthor on Instagram and as Sherry Ina on Facebook.

More gripping fantasies and thrillers from Sherlina Idid:

A) Mystical Adventure of Ashley Sprinkler

B) Today, Tomorrow & Never

C) New Adult Thriller: The Truth Unravel out in Qtr 1 2023

Made in the USA
Middletown, DE
28 June 2023